CW00547758

A ball of tenderness

Gérard Cavanna

A ball of tenderness
Novel

LE LYS BLEU
ÉDITIONS

© Lys Bleu Éditions – Gérard Cavanna

ISBN : 979-10-377-4303-9

Traduction : Koffi Anselme Kouadio

By the same author

Mom is gone
A son facing Alzheimer's disease
Saint Honoré Éditions – 2018

The Predator
The journey of a predator, from Syria to France
Saint Honoré Éditions - 2018

The Predator II The shadow of the copy-cat
Account settlements under the mark of the predator
Saint Honoré Éditions – 2019

Uprising on the Vth Republic
Revolt of the Yellow Caps
Pamphlet libertarian on the power in place
Le Lys Bleu Éditions – 2019

Foreword

The love and joy felt between a master and his favorite animal are at the heart of this French regional tour.

It is the unconditional love of an animal, this living being who gives you a look full of tenderness despite all your faults, your mood swings, which makes that one day you caress him and another time you send him to the corner.

Nevertheless, your honey ball corner back to you, wagging his little tail with tears in his eyes wondering what could have caused this fury, and what could be his fault!

But don't worry, you can torture him, cuddle him, ignore him, he is your companion, your friend, he will forgive you everything and will come back to you, full of love and sweetness, begging only for caresses and cuddles.

Chapter I
Julius, the Jack Russell

The Ushuaïa studios on the Quai du Point du Jour in Boulogne, a town in the Hauts-de-Seine, buzzed like a beehive, on this Monday in January 2015. Journalist Alex Callagan, specialized in animal reports, was convened by the great chief Christophe.

— Here is Alex, do an investigation on the relationship between a pet and its owner, in various regions in France. The passion that the French have with their dogs and cats deserves that we take an interest in them.

Give me something concrete, love, loyalty, all the sensations we can feel in front of our four-legged friends.

Alex grated in his beard, as usual he had to first look for a cheap hotel in the area where he had decided to start his investigations. The fixed daily rate that he had been given imposed him certain restrictions.

The Hauts-de-France was perfect for his first investigation, the hospitality of the people of the north was world-renowned, and Alex, passing through the area of Lille and Béthune, often saw animals running free in the streets. Edmée de Xhavée wrote *"who loves the animals, loves the peoples"* an old adage that ideally suits this population. He decided to put down his roots in the Novotel Lens Noyelles located three kilometers from Hénin-Beaumont.

<>

A light rain of January soaked the pavement of this commune of the Pas de Calais in the Haut-de-France. Hénin-Beaumont woke up slowly on this Sunday morning. There was a time when the bells of the town hall rang every quarter of an hour, reminding a local song written during the Great War.

Now the domes of the town hall are quite silent and overhang the large Jean Jaurès square, where a few people stroll with their noses to the ground, pressing their steps.

A few streets away, the people of Hénin, wrapped in their coats, hurried past the Sainte-Marie church, unaware of the little drama taking place on the square in front of the Catholic building.

Jean, a homeless man known to the parishioners and lying on cardboard boxes on the ground in front of the big oak and wrought iron door, was giving birth to his little Jack Russell dog.

Luc, the local priest, was concerned about the repeated knocks on the big door of the church. He was finishing studying his next Sunday sermon that he was going to preach in front of his flock and, incensed, he wondered who was the olibrius who was disturbing him at this hour of the morning.

— My lord, my lord, hurry Marie my little dog has just had two adorable puppies and there is a lot of blood. What should I do? What will happen to my little Marie?

14

— Jean, I have already told you that we are not in the seventeenth century, and that the church no longer takes in the homeless.

Well, you are going to get in and have a bowl of soup and we are going to see what we can do.

◇

The Veterinary Clinic on Schweitzer Boulevard had just opened its doors for a weekend shift. Dr. Maryse Sembor was immersed in the week's invoices when the phone rang and disturbed her calculations

— Yes, this is Dr. Sembor, can I help you? Ah, it is you, Father. One of your parishioners is having trouble with his favorite animal.

— Yes Maryse, you are a beautiful person and you will be thanked for your kindness to my needy, be sure. But right now, I have a poor man named Jean to whom I sometimes provide a bed in my church. He has a Jack Russell dog who has just given birth to two puppies. Could you take him and his little family under your wing?

Maryse, a good Catholic, answered affirmatively:

— Bring-them-to-me!

◇

In one of the streets adjacent to the Veterinary Clinic stood a small building housing a single-parent family, Sandra Nicoll, a courageous mother, and her disabled son Enzo, stuck in his wheelchair.

The neighbors of Melusine Street knew well the little man stuck in his chair and his mother pushing him boldly on the broken sidewalks of the old city.

Because the little Enzo was in his period of revolt, towards his mother and the society, because he did not manage to express what he felt neither by the word, nor by the gestures, because his universe was fragmented by small unsatisfied needs, by tantrums followed by apathy, because his mother, from as far back as she can remember, her love for him was different from other children. The doctors, after examining his case, made this terrible revelation: your son is autistic!

Sandra's husband could not bear the handicap of his baby and fled to the other side of the world, without regret, in a pitiful attitude.

Enzo knew how to walk but sometimes, and especially today, he had decided that his legs would not carry him, and it was up to his mother to take care of it. The rain had stopped and a pale sun was trying to pierce the layer of cumulonimbus clouds falling on the city of Hénin. Enzo was celebrating his tenth birthday on this first day of January.

Ten years of deprivation and abnegation for Sandra, but also ten years of joy and happiness at each moment of progress on the walk, the gestures of intelligence, the first words not stammered, the first sensible glimmers of understanding.

Yesterday, Simone Delfond, the social worker, made her weekly visit and wondered about Enzo's regression, who had not wanted to meet her for two weeks. They had established a certain connivance that had abruptly ended, without any reason.

On the eve of his birthday, Enzo had gone into a frightful rage. Sandra and Simone had talked about it for a long time and they had come to the conclusion that maybe he wanted to share his party with friends.

Easier said than done, Enzo often threw terrible tantrums that intimidated and scared away many of the kids.

— Why don't you find him a four-legged friend? Animal-assisted therapy or zootherapy refers to the set of non-conventional therapeutic methods that use the proximity of a domestic animal or pet to help a person suffering from disorders caused by his or her illness and to reduce stress, says Simone.

— That's a great idea, said Sandra, I will start looking for a puppy or kitten tomorrow.

Two weeks had passed and Sandra and Enzo had scoured the local kennels without finding the right one for their son. The cats were too independent and seemed suspicious of Enzo's autism, and the dogs were not to the kid's liking.

Two months had passed, but no animals had come into their lives, and their lives had resumed in fits and starts. As a good Catholic, Sandra asked Enzo:

— Since midnight mass on Christmas Eve, we haven't attended Father Luke's sermons. We will be going to church this Sunday, my darling, I hope that's okay?

When they arrived on the square of the church Sainte-Marie, the eternal trio of bigots were happily talking about the latest gossip of the neighborhood, Sandra pushing a grumbling and bad-tempered Enzo. Jean the homeless man was sitting on his cardboard boxes and begging for money, at the goodwill of the people entering. Marie, his little Russell dog, was playing with her two puppies, and at a sign from Jean, she came back to curl up between her master's legs, followed by one of her puppies. The second one shot up like an arrow, zigzagging among the parishioners, and came to lick Enzo's hand, which was hanging nonchalantly from his armchair.

Sandra, who had just blocked the wheels of the wheelchair in the place dedicated to the disabled, was surprised at first and then delighted to see her Enzo who had just found his companion

The puppy's mischievous little face and his little tail trembling with excitement filled the boy with wonder. The puppy jumped on his lap as if he had understood the complicity between them.

Jean, who had just entered in search of the little dog, had tears in his eyes to see the happiness that emanated from these two beings who seemed to have been born to meet.

— I don't remember having seen this kind of encounter in my life... Excuse me my God for having blasphemed (*and he signs himself*) but I do not believe that my Julius; it is the name of my small dog, could find a better master!

Chapter II
Fripouille, the Australian shepherd

Alex had just left the Novotel in Hénin-Beaumont and remembered the different characters who had started his investigation, the priest Luc had helped him to dust off the story of the young autistic boy Enzo.

Brittany would be his second anchorage point. He put down his bags in a hotel relay, Le Bigouden in Guilvinec.

<>

At the other end of France, in the department of Pyrénées-Orientales, a storm warning was broadcast on local radio stations, France Bleu Roussillon on 101.6 MHz.

"Red alert - Violent wind".

With its one hundred and thirty-six days of tramontana in the year and peak winds of one hundred and fifty kilometers per hour, Perpignan knows the risks inherent in the sudden outbursts of the god Aeolus, and knows how to protect itself, by inviting the people of Perpignan to take shelter.

In the premises of the SPA shelter, the staff was calming down the most sensitive animals. It was a visiting day, so some families discovered the cats and dogs in their prison universe. The cages were very airy and spacious enough for the well-being of the animals waiting to find a place in their future family.

A couple of Bretons, Erwan and Gwenaëlle Briec, tried to please their little girl Gaëlle, by taking her to see *"four-legged plushies"* as she defined them so well. Originally from Guilvinec, a small coastal town in Finistère, the Briec family was known and appreciated by all. Gwenaëlle was a teacher in the kindergarten of the rue du Château and Erwan lived from his music, animating weekend dances in the region's balls. They were not rich, but a baby of love had entered their home, a little more than eleven years ago, in this wonderful little girl, Gaëlle.

Erwan adored his daughter and always began his repertoire of songs with a tribute to Gaëlle

"When you arrived All the angels were singing I gave you your very first kiss You will give me
And you'll probably give me your last."[1]

All three of them had their lives figured out like clockwork, until that awkward time when the dark clouds seemed to gather on their heads.

It started with heat, fatigue, loss of appetite, abdominal pain and repeated vomiting, until the appalling diagnosis *"your daughter has cancer.*

When they named the cancer *"leukemia"*, the doctors explained that the normal blood cells in their daughter's bone

---

[1] Leah, song by Dany Brillant.

marrow was replaced by cancer cells. The symptoms of the disease included anemia, a decrease in leukocytes and platelets.

The Briecs scoured the hospitals in Brittany in search of the best practitioners to treat their Gaëlle's leukemia.

They stopped at the University Hospital of Rennes specialized in this type of cancer.

The first six months of chemotherapy were hellish for their daughter. Like a good soldier, she was led into the therapy rooms, where she was showered with serums, chemo sessions, and advice that was either useless or helpful, depending on what she said.

The first hair loss was terrible for a preteen conscious of her emerging femininity.

Once again she decided to put her hair down *"Kojak style"* and wear a bandana.

One evening when she was vomiting her guts, Erwan found her diary, hidden under her pillow

"I have just seen my parents crying their eyes out, and heard them mortgage their small house to pay for my medical care, I would like to die and not endure the suffering this disease" inflicts on me anymore.

Erwan gently put his daughter's precious treasure back in its place, more convinced than ever to care for his child.

During a period of intensive care at the University Hospital of Rennes, Erwan came across a ten year old boy with a puppy in his arms, with a smooth head and no hair, in the corridors of the children's cancer ward. The child opened his big hazel eyes and started a conversation:

— Hello sir, my name is Gaz, short for Gaspard, I can see from your colored bracelet that you have come to see a sick child?

— Yes, I accompany my daughter Gaëlle,

— Ah the little leukemia girl, I love her, we often talk about our dark future, I have this kind of disease myself, and we got closer to compare our results. Apparently, her leukemia is less aggressive than mine, and she should be out on leave soon.

"On leave?"

— Yes, when we have a period of remission, the doctors let us take a few days of freedom with our family, it's a bit like in the army; if we are kind and don't make any trouble, we get a leave.

— And tell me Gaz, what is this cute little dog?

— He is an Australian shepherd, his eyes are of different colors which makes him rare. But don't think I chose him, he adopted me.

I was walking with my parents in a kennel for abandoned animals, when I stopped in front of a cage where there were several puppies of the same breed.

Fripouille, that's the name he agreed, I offered him several and he selected this one. So he was in his corner and did not move. My parents knew that I had wanted a dog of this breed for some time, when the door of the cage was opened, all the other little Australian shepherds went back to the back as if they were listening to an order coming from somewhere else and Fripouille turned around and looked me straight in the eyes and I assure you, I thought I saw a blissful smile on his lips.

He stood up awkwardly on his paws, waddled over to me and jumped into my arms. Burying his muzzle in my neck, he licked me as if he was experiencing a supreme nirvana.

22

Since then, he is my little companion and he doesn't leave me for a second.

Gaëlle is too fragile now, but you should find her a little animal to keep her company.

Erwan went to Gaëlle's room and found his wife Gwenaëlle who had taken a year off to take care of their little girl.

Gaëlle was connected by pipes to a chemotherapy system, it was her last session and she had to leave the hospital for a short week of parental leave.

Erwan took his wife aside and asked about the conversation he had had with Gaz. They were going to spend this week looking for a companion for their beloved Gaëlle.

It had been a week that the Briec family was prospecting the SPA shelters of the Atlantic coast, without Gaëlle being enthusiastic about a small animal.

— Mom, dad, when I see Gaz and Fripouille, their complicity, their love, I am afraid I will never acquire this wonderful symbiosis.

— Don't lose hope my dear, says Gwenaëlle, there are so many animals waiting for a master, we will end up finding your happiness.

Outside the elements were raging, the swirling winds were blowing the windsocks of the nearby Perpignan airport. The windows of the kennel were vibrating, and the clouds were spinning towards the west, as if pushed by an unspeakable fear.

Standing in a waiting room, Gaëlle was going over dark thoughts. She had been twice around the cages without detecting the crush that Gaz had suggested to her.

They had met by chance and had never left each other. The doctors had finally moved Gaz and placed him in Gaëlle's room. Even the social workers, reluctant at first, had finally admitted that this promiscuity could be beneficial for the children.

When Gaëlle had left Gaspard the week before, he had promised her that she would find her future companion sooner than she had hoped.

She had left with her heart full of optimism, and now she missed Gaspard, her friend.

She was lost in her thoughts, when the revolving door of the room opened on these two parents in tears:

— Your friend Gaspard has just died, my dear, we must go back to Rennes.

— NO, she cried, not him!

The return trip in the car rented by his parents was very painful and trying. The joy they felt at the beginning of their quest had been eradicated by this terrible news.

Erwan and Gwenaëlle were completely devastated, and wondered how Gaëlle would react to Gaspard's corpse. The doctors had warned them that a regression could occur and wipe out all the benefits of the current chemo.

In this mood, they entered the CHU of Rennes completely mortified. Gaspard's parents were waiting for them and they fell into their arms in total collapse.

— My dear, said Gaspard's father, addressing Gaëlle, our son had warned us of his imminent departure, as if he wanted our acceptance that he was leaving. Our little guy had a huge heart and courage. He knew long before the doctors that he was going to join his grandparents, and it was he who comforted us.

There is also something that N must know Gaëlle, our son bequeaths you his little friend Fripouille. Gaz told me that it was Fripouille who asked him for this favor.

I don't know if this puppy will accept you, as he was very attached to Gaz.

Our son also asked me to let you into his room alone, do you think you can do that? She nodded after looking at her parents and went in to join her friend.

Gaspard seemed to be sleeping in his little white bed, with many flowers scattered around his coffin. On a chair in a basket, a little ball of fur seemed to be sleeping.

Animated by who knows what instinct, Fripouille looked up and saw Gaëlle, he jumped from his basket onto Gaz's corpse, went to lick his lips, seeming to say goodbye to him and with a pirouette rushed into Gaëlle's arms.

Erwan and Gwenaëlle in the corridor, were comforting Gaz's parents as best they could.

The four of them were wondering what Gaëlle would experience at the sight of her friend Gaz and about the continuation of his illness.

The door of the burial chamber opened and Gaëlle came towards them, Fripouille in her arms

— It is extraordinary, the room is filled with my friend Gaspard. I felt vibrations that made me shiver, as if he was talking to me. He suggested me not to worry about him, because he has passed into a heavenly world without pain, that he has joined his grandfather and soon his grandmother. And above all, to project into the future, a little brother or sister that I could contemplate from my cloud, in order to send you all three all my love.

Chapter III
Mélodie, the She-cat

Alex finished writing his Breton trip with tears in his eyes, he hoped to translate the melodrama he had just experienced with Gaëlle.

His next trip would take him to the east of France, to the Campanile de Bressey-sur-Tille near Dijon.

<>

In this particularly rainy month of January, the town of Bressey-sur-Tille in the Cote d'Or department was under water.

— The city was a victim of the overflow of the Gourmerault, a tributary of the Tille which is overloaded, explained Patrick Moineau the mayor.

Many Bresseyliens used to go to their homes by boat, escorted by firemen. The last flood was in 2013 but was nothing like it, the damage is likely to be in the thousands of euros. Never before in thirty years!

The Rateau family, father Yvan, mother Cyndie and their son Sam, had already returned to their home in the lower part of

Bressey, wrapped in life jackets and grouped in a fishing boat lent by the town hall.

— I wonder in what condition we will find our pavilion today, wondered Yvan

— It was a nightmare night, remember the garage was flooded to a height of five feet, the car was completely submerged, continued Cyndie.

— I remember an inky black sky with lightning bolts, I've never been so scared in my life, says Sam.

Luckily the town hall lent us a gym where we were dry, we could sleep on cots and we met up with the neighbors and my friends. It was great, it reminded me of camping in Baule!

— Yes, mumbled Yvan, don't think you're going to be on vacation, if the schools are closed, your mother will make you revise your homework.

— Pffff!

— Fortunately the river started to flow back. We arrive, hold you well we are going to accost and to benefit from the last hours of clearness to throw a glance on the damage of water, worried Cyndie. We took flashlights because, there is no electricity.

In single file, they opened the front door of their home, which, swollen with moisture, creaked with an ominous sound.

The elevation of their home had prevented the interior from flooding, and the place looked dry. Except for a lingering smell of miasma and mud in the air, one could assume that their home had escaped the worst.

A cathedral-like silence reigned in the place quickly broken by Sam's little voice

— Mom, I'm hungry!

28

— Listen, you both interrupted Yvan, we must first check if there was no damage and theft by marauders, as the city hall specified!

You Sam you look if your PlayStation is still in your room, ha ha, he said laughing, Cyndie and I will take a look at the important things.

Sam went up to his room, where nothing had moved, suddenly he stopped dead in his tracks. A strange noise was coming from the attic. He could hear the comforting voices of his parents coming from the first floor, and above his head in the attics, sliding and objects seemed to move on the floor.

He went down the stairs to the living room four by four and called out to his father

— Dad, there's someone rummaging in the attic, I have heard a noise!

— Name of name, I had left the skylight slightly open to eliminate the odors, admitted Cyndie.

— Well, I am taking my baseball bat and I am going to take care of their fate, Yvan said!

They went down the retractable staircase leading under the roof and Yvan climbed carefully the last steps, before resting on the joists of the attic.

It was dark as in an oven, or as in the pig's asshole as his grandmother used to say.

The place was cluttered with folding chairs, garden equipment and no sign of a human being where he could have hidden.

He made a 360° with his powerful lamp and aimed at a corner where there was movement.

He distinguished two phosphorescent eyes between two boxes that stared at him intently.

When he moved towards the animal, he discovered a large alley cat, which feared and spat at his approach.

He called his wife:

— Cyndie, it's a cat that has taken shelter from the weather, but it doesn't want me to go near it, come and see if you have better luck than me.

He fell back and Cyndie slowly walked towards the box where the mistigri was.

— Yvan, it is not a cat but a she-cat, who came to give birth to her babies. There were five of them but four died, only one kitten remains alive and she let me touch it. She is not at all shy, and I think we will adopt both of them, no both of them because they are both females.

A few months later, the Gourmerault had returned to its bed and Bressey-sur-Tille was licking its wounds. The insurance companies had been contacted and many depredations were still visible.

The Rateau family had grown with the arrival of the two she-cats, who had become friends especially with Cyndie, without anyone knowing why.

Two months after the kitten's weaning period, the she-cat disappeared overnight, as if she realized that her kitten was in good hands and that she could go back to living her life as a stray cat.

Cyndie had named her Mélodie, because she often emitted melodious meows under the caresses of her mistress.

— You are my little ball of love, whispered from time to time Cyndie in Mélodie's ear; if one day I die, I want to be reborn as a little she-cat!

Yvan worked in a mechanical machining company in Chenove near Dijon and Cyndie was a nurse in the emergency room of the Dijon University Hospital.

Their summer holydays took place in the beautiful city of Sète where the great Brassens was buried. They would pitch their tent in the "Flots bleus" campsite on the road to Frontignan. The adults would meet in the evening for a drink and Sam would play the fool in the swimming pool, that year Mélodie followed them and also had the right to her sea bath.

Back in their fiefdom, the Rateau family had their eyes full of starfish, well tanned and relaxed, ready to start a new school year, when Cyndie's first health problems began.

A minor persistent headache made it difficult for her to do her chores, and the only therapy at such times was bed rest.

Cyndie, who had never been sick, became unrecognizable, unbearable with her entourage, only Melodie managed to reassure her.

It had been several days since Cyndie had lived a peaceful life without any health problems, she loved these moments of respite but dreaded the cracks that occurred in her head, without any warning.

Neither the MRI nor the scans from the hospital in Dijon had been able to determine where these symptoms came from.

This weekend started well, Yvan and Sam had cooked the barbecue in the garden, with Mélodie in their legs.

She had just taken a shower and was combing her hair in front of the bathroom mirror, when suddenly she saw her face distort, like in a horror movie.

Her vision blurred as her mouth hung down to the right, followed by a numbness in her right arm.

Immediately she shouted while stammering

— Yvan, come..., I'm doing... Stroke[2], call... firemen and... Samu... now!

The intensive care unit of the vascular and cerebral neurology departments of the Dijon hospital did everything possible to take care of their colleague Cyndie.

The head of neurology took Yvan aside

— Cyndie is my friend, and I'm part of your family so I'm not going to hide anything from you. Regardless of the type of stroke, chronic conditions significantly increase one-year mortality.

Fourteen and a half percent of patients die during hospitalization, sixteen percent within a month, and twenty-eight percent within a few years following the stroke.

The promptness of the rescue will be of great help to us, and I will set about it without delay. Don't worry, you are in the best care unit in the country, I will take special care of your wife.

---

[2] Cerebrovascular Accident

32

Three months later, as the holidays approached, Yvan, Sam and Mélodie came to pick up Cyndie.

Yvan pushed her in her wheelchair, as her recovery from the stroke was not going so well. She was still on her feet and her husband did not want to take any risks.

When she entered her home, a large banner hung across the dining room stating:

"Welcome to our beloved mother."

Big tears sprang from Cyndie's azure eyes and fell to the floor.

— You are loves and I wish I could help you more. My brain sends orders to my legs and arms to move, but I feel like I'm living in a slow-motion movie where every movement breaks down endlessly.

Fortunately my little cat Mélodie, continues to whirr her purrs to me while licking my earlobes. I have the impression that she appeared in my life, to make me endure all the hazards which despair me.

As spring approached, the Rateau family spent most of their days in and out of the hospital. The stroke had damaged many of the synapses in the connection of her neurons, which had eventually left her confined to her wheelchair.

Autumn arrived with its procession of magnificent colors of the Indian summer. The chestnuts and bistros in the garden, which had been Cyndie's joy, seemed dull to her now. She who used to love to go alone, to take pictures and smell the scents of the forest, to pick mushrooms, to jog in the surrounding countryside, had no taste for anything anymore.

Mélodie, the kitten looked at her mistress without understanding the afflictions they were going through. She often had the glance in the vague, lost in distant countries. That exasperated Yvan.

The vacations had been trying, who has never pushed a wheelchair in the sand, could understand the misfortunes of the family.
Only Sam was able to escape the discomfort in the camping pool with his friends. But he missed his mom, although he didn't show it, who swam like a fish and moped around in her chair. Since he was four years old, he was splashing around in the watery element, a few years later he liked to swim laps with his mom in the pool, but now that she was gradually moving away into an imaginary world, he was completely distraught.

Two years, then three passed as if in a slow motion movie. Cyndie was now confined to an electric chair, completely paralyzed but unfortunately aware of her condition.
Yvan had succeeded in obtaining the AAH[3] from the general council of the Cote d'Or department in the Burgundy-Franche-Comté region, whose assistance made it possible to pay the expenses necessary for his wife to remain at home in spite of her loss of autonomy.

She was still young and had just celebrated her forty-second spring! She felt plague-stricken, her friends had long since deserted the marital home. How to converse with a person paralyzed in his body, unable to pronounce a word and that the only blink of the eyelids allowed him to express himself?

---

[3] Disabled adult allowance

Her husband, always in love, surrounded his wife with a thousand attentions and the last important purchase he had made was an eye-controlled computer. The basic principle was relatively simple; signals close to infrared were emitted, producing reflections on the cornea.

These are filmed by cameras and the data were processed by algorithms allowing to know the position of the eyes.

Visual targets are then used to calibrate the movement of the eyelids.

So she could *"chatter"* with her family, she would blink at her PC and the words would magically appear on the screen.

Professor Jean Schwarz, head of neurology at the University Hospital of Dijon, was never discouraged from treating Cyndie. At least to find the cause of her profound illness.

When he managed to decipher the different symptoms and to establish a name for this form of disability, he began by bursting into tears, for a long, long time!

She was suffering from a syndrome with a nice name, almost an oxymoron "the LIS of death".

The Locked In Syndrome is the term used to designate the patient suffering from a tetraplegia and a damage of the last cranial pairs, by bilateral deterioration of the cortical-spinal ways but whose consciousness remains intact. He sees everything, hears everything but cannot move anything, because of a complete paralysis, except for the movement of the eyelids and the eyes. The cognitive faculties of the subject are on the other hand intact.

LIS is most often caused by a stroke, which destroys the bridge (a portion of the brain stem), the part of the central nervous system located inside the skull that serves as a passageway for nerves.

LIS is described as an *"internal confinement"* whose fatal outcome is punctuated by extremely painful moments.

Jean Schwarz stood in front of the Rateaux's home for several minutes, wondering how he was going to tell his friend this terrible news.

A curtain moved in the windows, and the son Sam ran out of the house and threw himself into John's arms.

— Godfather, you didn't tell us about your visit. Mom will be very happy!

His friendship with Cyndie began on the faculty benches. She was then his medical student, he was already the professor who had taken her under his wing. She was a high performer, above the rest, as he often said to her *"you will go far."*

He was the father who had replaced his father who had left too early from a devastating cancer. He lived alone, without any ties and when she asked him to be the godfather of her child, he gladly accepted. He was part of the family and today he was not coming to announce good news.

He often said :

We must not hide anything from the patients, even if the truth is difficult to hear, the patients must absorb it and know what will happen to them.

But now his fundamentals were being shaken to their foundations. How do you talk about it with your friend and family?

Jean entered the premises and immediately found the living room transformed into a medical room. The ground floor had become the area dedicated to Cyndie because of concerns about sleeping and moving the electric wheelchair.

On his right, he saw the electric lift bed with variable height which allowed the bed to be placed at ground level, ideal for a quadriplegic handicapped person.

On his left, a PC mounted on an easel with a large screen of about fifty inches for easier reading.

In front of him was poor Cyndie, forever immobilized in her chair, with her head bent over and staring at him with laughing, feverish eyes. She stood in front of her computer, and the words were written with speed on the monitor:

— My God, my friend, why don't you come more often, I miss you, we missed you a lot!

Even if you don't see it on my face, I have a huge smile on my face, an intense satisfaction in looking at you.

I don't have many visitors, people have abandoned me.

But I'm not going to sadden you with my moods, I'm happy, too happy to have you here.

Tell us what is the news from Dijon, and how are my colleagues doing?

— Cyndie my friend, I have to tell you about the evolution of your disease.

— Why are you turning your back on me, Jean? You have always been frank with me, straightforward, the raw truth, as you have always explained it to me.

LOOK AT ME! if I write you in capital letters, it is because I am shouting; TELL ME EVERYTHING!

And Jean turned, his eyes clouded with big tears

— My dear, you are like my daughter and I am going to explain to you what I have suspected for a long time.

You have contracted Locked In Syndrome, following your stroke. This syndrome makes you fully aware of your body and your environment, although you have no control over your limbs. You can locate them accurately in space and unlike patients paralyzed by a ruptured spinal cord, you can feel touch and pain.

Commonly referred to as LIS, this syndrome is known as motor deafferentation, locked-in or locked-out.

Well, at the moment you are in the primary phase of this syndrome. You breathe on your own and you are fed by tube, incontinence is part of the inconvenience of tetraplegia.

In the chronic phase, you will have to do chest physiotherapy for respiratory assistance.

"Could I still use my computer with my eye software?" wrote Cyndie feverishly.

"The patients who reached this last stage were in a terrible condition that required full hospitalization," Jean said, bursting into tears.

— And if I want to end my life, how do I go about it, euthanasia is forbidden in France if I am not mistaken?

— The courts have already condemned doctors who have put an end to the life of one of their patients. And you know that my ethics and my religious convictions forbid me to even consider it. I had an acute terminal cancer last year, the poor child was suffering the martyrdom as much as his parents.

I sent a complete file with photos and videos to the Medical Association, to the departmental health services, to the Minister of Health, and even to the President of the Republic, in order to find a solution and to put an end to the intolerable pain of this kid. Without any result.

To say that neighboring countries such as Switzerland or Belgium practice assisted suicide is to say that it is the act of providing an environment and the necessary means for a person to end their life, to commit suicide. Assisted suicide is different from euthanasia, it is the "patient" himself who initiates his death and not a third party... but I didn't tell you that.

Cyndie steered her chair towards a corner of the living room where Mélodie's bassinet was located. Mélodie meowed at her approach and sensing her mistress' upset, jumped onto her lap and buries his muzzle in the blondness of his hair. Humming like a seaplane.

When Jean left their home, carrying the weight of all the misery of the world on his shoulders, Yvan threw himself on his wife and kneeling down, wrapping his arms around her with infinite tenderness, said:

— My darling, we will face this together, remember *"in joy and sorrow"*, the priest had prayed to us during our wedding in the little church.

And he collapsed into burning blades, his head buried in his wife's blond hair next to Mélodie.

Yvan immediately set out to find the right place that would suit their funeral project. He stopped at a private hospital in Belgium called *"Arucipe"* which practiced legal euthanasia, authorized by Belgian law and decriminalized since 2002. Very well supervised in our Belgian neighbors, it is necessary that the pathology is incurable and that the physical and psychological suffering is unbearable for the patient.

The doctors who practice it have undergone a training called EOL[4], they accompany the patient for months, sometimes several years, before the euthanasia.

Together with his wife, they called to make a quick appointment with the head of the department Sergei Blicec.
A month later, the Rateaus arrived at the Arucipe Hospital in Ath, Belgium, half an hour from the French border. They found a large white building with large glass doors at the reception.
They followed the corridors of the neurology department, to a spacious office cluttered with green plants where Dr. Sergei Blicec received them without emphasis.

A patient, with a waxy cancer complexion, got up from a chair and gave the doctor a friendly pat on the shoulder
— Thank you doc' for all this instructive information, I return to my room.
Sergei Blicec answered with a few words, underlined by a brotherly smile.

---

[4] End of life

— Hello Yvan, hello Cyndie, did your trip go well? I received your file, sent by my eminent colleague Professor Jean Schwarz; no your file, here we are on familiar terms, we do not set up any barrier between doctor and patient.

We have the right to empathize with our patient, he explained, we necessarily create a link of follow-up because euthanasia is only the continuation of a treatment.

It is for this reason that it is practiced by the doctor who knows the patient. The therapeutic relationship is therefore fundamental.

France is still retrograde on this topic, it will come, like Belgium, because we must have the right to die with dignity without the suffering dedicated to the disease. It has given the right to abortion, the rest will follow.

We have an enormous power in our hands, to give death. Also, even surrounded, the whole health care team, the nurse, the occupational therapist, the physiotherapist must affirm its agreement and at that moment, you are alone to trigger the process.

In a corner of the office stood a PC on a tripod, with the eye movement software installed, Cyndie would be able to converse

"Hello professor, my job as a nurse has taught me to tell a patient's family that they are dying, but never to worry about my own departure.

Have you ever accompanied LIS patients to their EOL, well, here I am expressing myself in abbreviation, which I hate."

— Yes Cyndie, I have chaperoned several LIS patients. It is an abominable condition that locks the patients into their own suffering. The last patient with this syndrome was an English girl, whose parents fought with the British justice to have the right to euthanasia recognized, without any success.

I followed her for two years, in a much more advanced state than yours. She did not want to leave without her parents' acceptance, and they were not resigned to saying goodbye to their beloved little girl.

I had to explain to them the internal pains felt by this little girl, without them being able to observe her suffering. The smooth face, the lack of tears, the absence of gum contractions, the biting of the tongue, everything that we feel in the face of pain, she could not show.

And she did not want to leave without her beloved parents being in tune with her. Her last trip was marked by great dignity, despite her mother's nervous breakdown and screaming.

This little cutie marked my entire staff, and we decided not to accept any more EOL children in our department.

— But tell me, Yvan, what is this cradle that accompanies you?

— Ah, let me introduce you to Melody, my wife's lucky cat, replied the husband.

She entered in our life through one of the windows of our house, during the last floods of Bressey-sur-Tille. My son and I could not approach the animal, only Cyndie had the right to his favors, even now she lives and acts as a real watchdog for her mistress, she does not leave her a sole or rather a pad.

Mélodie is unbearable when Cyndie has to do exams so we take her every time.

— Yes, "the professor enthused," pet therapy is an excellent approach to dealing with your wife's misfortunes.

— We named her Mélodie, because from time to time she sings or rather she emits musical and harmonious meows which calm the troubles of her mistress.

Every day she surprises us with her immeasurable love for her mistress. The number of mice and sparrows that this cat deposits in front of the wheelchair, like a maternal gift, indicates this mark of unconditional affection that she carries to her.

Lately she even saved his life...

— What do you mean?

— This is an anecdote that I like to tell, even if it strongly displeases my wife! It happened during our last vacations at the Camping des Flots Bleus in Sète where we had rented a mobile home. Our son Sam spent his days at the swimming pool with his friends, while I took part in the sports activities of the camp, archery, petanque, soccer.

My wife wandered around in her electric wheelchair with Mélodie trotting by her side. From time to time, she would stop by the pool to admire Sam's dives. In short, we were having a happy vacation, as much as we could.

While Mélodie, with her specific character of cats, accepted our caresses with a disdainful air, a way of saying, I am at home here and I accept you because you are part of my mistress' family, but don't ask me more!

She never came to purr on our knees, she didn't beg anything from Sam and me, she put up with us and that's all.

All this to explain you the context of our current life and of this privileged vacation between Cyndie and Mélodie.

Also, when this cat jumped on my bed, early one morning, looking at me with a panicked air, the hair bristling on the back, I felt an imminent drama.

She jumped out of bed and turned around on the doorstep of my room, looking at me as if to say "hurry the fuck up"!

She took off like an arrow and I ran behind her to the silent pool at four in the morning.

Melody leaned over the edge and as I approached, I saw my wife in her chair, at the bottom of the water, looking at me with an angry expression! I dived and I brought her up, I had arrived in time, thanks to this little she-cat who jumped with joy and licked her mistress with her shrinking tongue.

She had tried to commit suicide by guiding her chair into the dark waters of the pool.

— Today, we have passed a milestone, Yvan continued, I don't want to shiver by not knowing what is going on in my wife's head.

Cyndie moved her chair, meaning that she wanted to take part in the conversation

"I would like to know the process that will await me when I am ready to leave, she exclaimed, can you explain to me in detail, dear professor?"

Yes, my dear Cyndie, that day we will place you under a drip, which will allow the injection of a strong dose of anaesthetic products, then curare which will provoke a total paralysis, then a crescendo of sleep and, if necessary, potassium chloride for the final phase.

Depending on the patient's wishes, euthanasia can take five minutes or twenty-four hours. Some people want to extend the passage to this famous light by falling asleep surrounded by their loved ones.

For many, it is unbearable to depend on a third party to die with dignity. And finally, very few go through with the process, because the alternative of palliative care is always possible.

— I remember a seventy-eight year old administrator of property, of strong character, who had built up a personal fortune, living alone but not wanting to become dependent on anyone.

This person had come to see me, determined to end his earthly life, which was weighing too heavily on him. He had made all the transfers of his fortune to charity, the most beautiful women in the world had passed through his bed, but his infertility had not allowed him to experience the joys of fatherhood.

He wanted nothing more than to leave.

Last week I found him very sad, very different from the character he had built up, so the decision must not be due to a temporary depression, we have an excellent psychiatric service that put him back on track, and ultimately refuse the final act.

This sadness was a part of the disease that we can treat.

We never propose euthanasia, the request comes from the patients who imperatively ask for it.

Pain and death are not part of medical training. The idea of Christ's redemptive suffering is instilled in us from childhood: "You will give birth to children in pain". These are the words spoken and instilled in us by our ancestors, who have shaped our convictions.

Therapeutic persistence is not part of our priesthood, the dignity of the patient will always be preserved.

Thus a report is submitted to the Commission of Control and Evaluation which can intervene after the fact. It was set up during the law of decriminalization of 2002.

Less euthanasia is practiced than before and for the better.

A few years ago it was hidden, we were going off the beaten track, now the law preserves us from any state of mind, we are within the law [5].

Until the last moment, you can say: NO.

Here Cyndie, I have prepared a room for you, where you can rest and think about other questions, and talk to me at any time about anything!

Days went by, weeks and months, and Cyndie had started a novel about her life, or at least what was left of it.

The first hundred pages were written in a flash, she felt that soon her eyes would no longer be able to obey her and write on her computer at her convenience.

She had so many nice things to say, but also some nasty things to say about institutions that forget about the disabled and leave their families to deal with their problems alone.

She covered several pages on the dependence of the sick and the caregivers who often take care of their sick relative, unable to move, at the cost of their own life.

All this had a cost, both financial and human. State aid is too low and often not harmonized with the needs of the people.

---

[5] Report "The Voice of the North".

She didn't want to let too much bitterness or gall show in her writing, so she took up several passages with much more lightness.

Her husband Yvan helped her when her memories were fraying and fatigue was keeping her on her desk.

Mélodie brought her moral and musical comfort, from time to time she modulated new sounds, subjective meows as if to give her courage when Cyndie was struggling on a blank page.

The little cat jumped mischievously on her knees and hid in the folds of her dress, looking for the scent of her mistress, her little face sticking out of her bodice.

She had been looking for a few days for a punch line that would finalize her story, both pathetic and joyful, almost an oxymoron.
She imagined it by remembering a François Truffaut film that she had enjoyed at the cinema-
"The woman next door[6]" where the hero was subjugated by his neighbor, this story ended tragically for both protagonists. She ended her book with:
"Never with my life, never without my life".
She had also found a title that would ring true to her ears:
"My sublime imprisonment".
His will was to leave a memory of his painful and desperate existence, dictated by a fierce thirst for life, and this could be felt in his writings.

---

[6] The woman next door, 1981 film with Gérard Depardieu and Fanny Ardant

Yvan had sent his manuscript to Belgian and French publishers when his health suddenly deteriorated.

Yvan thought for a long time that Cyndie had gone beyond her strength to finish her novel.

His wife uttered a tragic phrase on her teleprompter:
"It's time, my love, call the professor!"

Sergei Blicec entered the room, his eyes misty behind his glasses

— I've just read a few pages of your novel, Cyndie, I'm sure it will be a bestseller, and I'll be your first reader, my dear!

I have arranged a cozy room for you, full of orchids, the flower you like best.

Through the French window, you will be able to observe nature, the trees caramelizing in this autumn season, the one you also like, there are two beds for Yvan and Sam, as well as a pretty bassinet chosen by the hospital team, for Mélodie.

During these two years that we spent together, I had all the time to express my deep admiration for what you endure and for your manuscript that will perhaps allow to change the laws on euthanasia in France.

The next twenty-four hours were horrifying for Yvan and Sam, the process had begun and there was no turning back.

Sergei and the caregivers were taking turns with their every wish.

Only Mélodie had not moved from her crib and nobody could understand her.

Cyndie's death occurred during the night of Saturday to Sunday, when Yvan and Sam were too exhausted and asleep on their beds.

Sergei Blicec came to make the usual observations with his stethoscope and turned off the monitors that had been beeping for the last few hours.
Everyone surrounded Cyndie who seemed to be asleep, Yvan spoke up.
— There is something missing, but I don't see what? Sergei walked towards the bassinet.
— I know, I can't hear Mélodie's meows. He bent over the little basket and got up with tears in his eyes, the little she-cat is dead too, I just checked her, she joined her mistress in death!

Cyndie was buried in the small cemetery of Magny-sur-Tille, with a large committee. Yvan, Sam, Jean Schwarz and Sergei the professor, as well as the staffs of the hospitals of Dijon and Arucipe.

In Yvan's car was a small coffin with Mélodie's name in gold letters.

On the internet, he had asked a very important question, could he bury his wife with her favorite little animal.

The answer was negative
"By virtue of articles L.2223-3 and L.2223-13 of the general code of territorial communities, burial in a communal graveyard is due to persons only." The mayor cannot therefore authorize the burial of an animal or its ashes in the grave or vault with a deceased person.

He took advantage of the fact that the gravediggers had turned their backs to delicately deposit the small box like a treasure near Cyndie.

Yvan imagined them both gambolling in Valhalla, without constraints of armchair, Mélodie meowing of happiness and Cyndie laughing to the bursts.

A few weeks later, a novel appeared on Amazon and the Fnac *"My sublime imprisonment"* announced as the future Best-Seller of the year.

Chapter IV
Hope, the Little Tiger

Cyndie and Mélodie are marked in golden letters in Alex's mind. He hoped to have transcribed with precision the last moments of the little she-cat, the favorite animal of this sublime woman.

After having settled the last details at the hotel Campanile,

He looked at the map of France, Lozère stood out from the other departments. This would be his next objective.

In the Monts d'Ardèche Regional Natural Park, the skies seemed to be unleashed. A thunderstorm streaked the sky and drifted towards the village of Langogne. Located in the department of Lozère in the Occitanie region, at the limit between the Haute-Loire and the Ardèche, the village was undergoing the jolts of an autumn weather.

The Bonzini circus had just finished setting up the big top, and securing the tensioners to pitons deeply embedded in the ground of the meadow, kindly lent by the mayor Gilles Gensac.

Cantonese festivities were rare and the inhabitants tended to flee to the big cities. When an event could attract and amuse the crowds and in particular the children, it was not to be missed.

Under the canvas of the tent, which was shaking on its seams, lower down on the artists' ring, the employees were struggling to put up the bleachers that would allow the future spectators to sit and admire the performances of the acrobats, clowns, and animals.

Charles Bonzini, the owner, often complained that speciesists and other vegans were abusing his menagerie and cages.

Some thought that the cloistered animals were unhappy and wanted their freedom.

Charles retorted that his animals were better cared for than in the wild, and that in the jungle they kill each other, cripple each other, fight, when it is not the poachers, the predators who hunt them.

In his circus they are heated, they eat their fill, they are medically treated and they show themselves off in front of a crowd that applauds them, and there they act like clowns[7] and find their own satisfaction.

To a journalist from Ouest-France, he argued.

— Look at my chimpanzees, my trainer raised them on a bottle, they put on their tutus and run around the ring doing their somersaults.

---

[7] Show off, seek attention

My Transylvanian cubs jump rope and even hoops with grace, the camels jabber among themselves and it is not under the blows.

We have just had a birth, a little tiger which is a hybrid of a lioness and a tiger, something that you never come in the wild, because the lion and the tiger have radically opposite behaviors and habitats.

The little tiger is a small female that we named "Hope", or rather my grandson Claudio was in charge of finding a good-sounding name for her, so this little ball of fur is well named in French "Espoir".

When he was born, the lioness did not want us to approach him, she and the tiger his father had placed him in the bottom of the cage and made a wall with their massive bodies.

The tiger was snarling and the lioness was snarling and showing her fangs, and we were wondering how to give first aid to the little tiger.

And the miracle happened. One day, as my son was walking past the cage, we saw the couple of animals approaching the bars and rubbing against them, a way of saying *"we like you, come and see us!"*

The little tiger moved awkwardly on its little legs to the opening of the cage and Claudio was able to seize it without a blow. Since then he takes care of Hope like a second mother.

Claudio will soon celebrate his fifteenth birthday but he is paralyzed in a wheelchair after an acrobatic accident. My four children, from the moment they were born, were children of the ball, and my grandchildren too. They could ride and do acrobatics before they could walk.

Claudio fell about ten meters from a trapeze and the net bounced him on the track. Doctors say that his paralysis is psychosomatic and that if he wanted to, he could walk.

May his motor functions be intact, but I believe that apprehension makes him doubt. We travelers know how to take care of our own, come what may, he will always know my grandson.

At the end of the week, the weather was more clement, the sky was clear and a pale sun was beginning to appear.

The streets of Langogne resounded under the passage of a Toyota Pick-up in the colors of the Bonzini circus. A big loudspeaker placed on the roof of the cab announced the program of the evening. On the back platform, clowns were clowning around, handing out candy and flyers to children on the sidewalks.

— Ladies and Gentlemen, come and see our acrobats, our artists, our animals, they are waiting for you with impatience to entertain you.

Charles Bonzini was at the wheel of the Pick-up and was reeling off his advertising speech, the population was beginning to peek in the windows, the shutters were opening on amused eyes, the evening promised to be beautiful.

In the alleys of the circus, it was not yet the hour of the representation, between the caravans all a small world swarmed, there a juggler threw hoops in the air and caught them adroitly, further two clowns fought gaily with pirouettes and enormous bursts of laughter, An elephant accompanied by his mahout strolled along, shaking the ground under his heavy step, a marmoset dressed as a hotel bellboy with his red cap jumped on his trainer's shoulders, all of them headed towards the big top.

Today we were celebrating a surprise birthday, Claudio's birthday. He had just got out of his caravan, which had been specially adapted for the disabled, and his wheelchair with a special access ramp. Hope the little tiger was now six weeks old and was proudly running around with his master.

Claudio had advantageously replaced his mother the lioness, who was now ostensibly uninterested in him.

He had waited for the weaning of the lioness and continued to feed him with a bottle, like a baby. The tigron had the almond-shaped eyes of the felines and the grace of the tigers in his movements.

Her paws were extended by knife-sharp claws, and when she smiled her carnivorous teeth showed impressive mini fangs.

A clown who wanted to get too close to Claudio, had received a masterly blow of the paw "don't touch, friend" seemed to say Hope.

For some time now, Otto the wild animal trainer had been taking in hand the young tigon, who one day would be in performance as well.

Hope was unbearable under Otto's whip, and one could guess the aggressiveness of the tiger under its apparent passivity.

— Achtung, the trainer exclaimed, Hope is going to be a big problem, today it weighs thirty kilos, tomorrow two hundred kilos, unmoglichzugehorchen[8]

— Take it easy Otto, he replied, I'll leave Hope to you, Charles my father has asked me to go to the marquee.

Claudio spun the wheels of his chair and moved quickly down the aisle. He knew Hope was in good hands.

Even as a young boy he had watched Otto tame the animals in German, a guttural language made for command. And yet he was 1.60 meters tall, all muscle, but when he gave a command the beasts lay down and did not move... impressive.

The strange silence in the alleys and the lack of people around the caravans should have given him a hint, but when he passed the tent's airlock, a huge clamor sounded:

"Happy birthday, Claudio."

All the people of the circus were there, some had tears in their eyes, especially Charles who had a share of responsibility in his fall from the trapeze.

Despite this, everyone surrounded him and the guitars started the gypsy songs, clapping their hands as only gypsies know how.

The afternoon passed like a dream for Claudio, having received his share of gifts and happiness.

Soon the show will start in the evening:

"The show must go on."

All the artists were getting ready and putting on their light clothes, ready to perform their act as if their lives depended on it.

---

[8] Today it weighs thirty kilos, tomorrow two hundred kilos, difficult to obey

Luigi and Barbarella, held a small stand near the tent, of candy, cotton candy, churros, grilled corn, during the intermissions she wandered between the benches of the spectators, offering sweets and treats to children.

Divine and feline, she escaped the wandering hands of some men who wanted to rub her charms.

Luigi, her husband, was doing a trapeze show high above the heads of the amazed and delighted public.

Italian and jealous, he watched from the corner of his eye Barbarella circulating lower between the spans laughing and laughing at the dirty jokes of young teenagers. She knew her power of seduction and used and abused it.

With her husband watching over her, he would give her a beating in the evening and she loved it.

Luigi didn't forget that he had been the cause of the drama during the training with Claudio, had he intentionally let him down?

At the dawn of his sixteenth year, Charles' grandson was wall-to-wall for his age and the girls in the circus were all over him, and often ended up in his bed. Among the gypsies, boys become men quickly and women give birth as soon as they are thirteen.

Then when Barbarella addressed magnificent smiles to Claudio, Luigi mumbled and resumed his jealousy in silence. Had he unconsciously caused the fall of the outfielder?[9]

---

[9] Among trapeze artists, there is the carrier and the acrobat.

Without witness, nobody could incriminate Luigi, only the little tiger did not accept his presence and she scolded when he approached his master, seeming to sense his bad intentions

— I didn't do anything to your mini-wild friend, he declared, calm him down before an accident happens!

— Hope is the star at the moment, people come especially to see her, don't approach her by surprise, she won't do you any harm, especially if you are kind to me!

Well, I'll leave you, I'm going to go to the second part of the show soon, let's not make our public wait.

Luigi went to his booth, where some people were already waiting for him. From where he stood, he could hear Charles dressed as Mr. Loyall[10] presenting the next entertainment:

— Ladies and gentlemen, here is Claudio accompanied by Hope his little tiger, you will not find this animal in the wild since it is the crossing of the lioness Clarence and our tiger Shere Khan, two beasts not living in the same part of the world.

I ask you to give them a tremendous ovation... all of a sudden, a noise rose from inside the tent.

Luigi was following from the corner of his ear, the wheelchair shining with a thousand lights for the show, Claudio dressed as a trainer, a beast skin on his shoulders, in his right hand a whip snapping in the air and Hope firing with each "schlackk" showing her fangs.

---

[10] Master of the circus ring, chief entertainer.

The lap was almost over, and the applause was growing louder, an OLA had started in the corner of the room entertainer[11] Hassan.

Luigi could see on the outside of the tent canvas, the wave moving as people got up and touched the tent. He suspected that Hassan have had an affair with Barbarella without having any proof. Just thinking about it, he hit his cotton candy machine, making myriads of multicolored threads fly.

Argh, well for that, tonight she was going to take!

The third part of the show was about to begin, with the trapeze artists twirling in the air.

Luigi had put on his sequined spindle and warmed up in his caravan. He arrived on the dance floor wearing a white cape with a gold trim. A rope fell from the infrastructure and he climbed up, proud of his abs.

Tonight, he had decided to modify some of his flights. Several times in training, he had attempted the quadruple jump from death, without success. He had warned his "carrier" and also Charles for the presentation that would make him rise in the hierarchy of "impossible quadruple jumps".

In the meantime, he grabbed the lanyard and moved the steps of the platform to launch himself from higher up and to have a better momentum.

---

[11] Entertainer, public animator.

He looked at the audience, thirty meters below, his clown buddies were white and not just under their make-up.

People were shaking with fear, some women were signing, others were hoping in their heart of hearts to see the acrobat crash to the ground.

Barbarella, his wife, was shaking her head, expressing her disappointment at her husband's stupidity in trying to impress the gallery again.

The orchestra fell silent and only the drums began a continuous roll, announcing an upcoming feat. The people held their breath, the children opened their eyes wide, even the animals in their cages laid down their ears, sensing that death was near.

Claudio, seeing the scene, felt the hairs on the back of his neck stand up, even Hope had crossed her paws over her head.

Malik, the carrier, chalked up his hands and forearms with magnesia, dashed forward and recovered from a caper, finding himself head down with arms flailing, ready to catch his partner.

Luigi, full of grandiloquence, waved to the audience and leapt into the void, holding his trapeze bar tight.

Hundreds of eyes followed the acrobats' circumnavigations, waiting to count Luigi's four turns.

— ONE, TWO, THREE, FOUR relayed by hundreds of votes, the count went to the end of the four rounds.

From his armchair, Claudio counted down the tricks like the crowd, watching the scene like in a slow motion movie, imagining himself in Luigi's place, the adrenaline that ran through the veins of these artists was intense and allowed them to sublimate themselves.

Unfortunately, a bad synchronization prevented Malik from landing Luigi well, who fell like a dead leaf into the big safety net.
A big *"HOOO"* went through the audience who remained silent without any claps.

A huge burst of laughter resounded during Luigi's recovery on the dance floor, was it a nervous breakdown or hilarity, Barbarella was still laughing under her breath, when Luigi came towards her and gave her a tremendous slap that sent her flying down the aisles, among the spectators.

A woman got up from her seat screaming, her hands full of blood, at her feet lay Barbarella with a bloody head.

Several spectators held a furious Luigi, preventing him from blowing up Barbarella.
Charles and several men dragged him away and put him in a cage to calm him down.
Hopefully the next game would be entertainment with the clowns Grock and Dimitri.

A missed number was nothing, it could happen, but a slaughter as it had just happened was unbearable for the business. He left to join Luigi, finally reassured.
— You know what brings me here, said Charles.

— Yes, I was a jerk, I flipped out, I screwed up my jump, he apologized

— You have no excuse, everywhere we go you make a mess, you will pay the consequences, you're fired!

Barbarella can stay if she wants, you're not married under our traditions, you take your gear and go, the candy stand belongs to me, you'll leave only bad memories. Ciao !

The news spread like wildfire, the bad boy Luigi was out. Many said they understood the boss Bonzini, others regretted it. But everyone was happy, the acrobat had hurt everyone too much.

Barbarella's face was swollen from falling on a bench. She had decided to stay, there was still a place in Claudio's caravan, which was good timing.

The night looked peaceful and cloudless, the circus and the bodies rested, the weather forecast good weather the next day.

A burning smell tickled Hope's nostrils, she raised her mouth to her lips and groaned.

Barbarella was stunned by the meds and slept in the back of the room.

Claudio had gone out and dined at his grandfather's, across the camp.

Hope guessed that the fire had caught under the caravan, he had to warn his little master. She jumped through the ajar window and lila at Charles' house. In front of the caravan, she roared as loud as she could, and the door opened to Claudio, who sensed misfortune when she saw Hope alone. He turned around and saw smoke coming from his trailer.

The little tiger leaps on his knees and nestles under his sweater, panicked by the hints of smoke.

Claudio realized that he could never arrive in time to save Barbarella, sitting in his chair. With a superhuman effort, he got up and his legs supported him as if by miracle.

He advanced, put one step in front of the other, trotted and ended up running.

He opened his caravan, and took the young woman asleep in his arms. On the doorstep, turning around, he saw Luigi the renegade pointing a gun in his direction

— How many times do we have to try to make you disappear, to succeed? I won't be able to have my Barbarella anymore, but neither will you, and he fired, just as Hope was pounding his paws and claws out.

His mouth closed on the throat of Luigi who collapsed, the trachea torn from a sheaf of blood.

The bullet had not touched him and Claudio understood what had happened when he saw his Hope, the coat spotted with carmine red.

She had made the supreme sacrifice of her life to save her master, receiving death.

Chapter V
Neige, the German Shepherd

Alex finished his paragraph where Hope the tigon had thrown himself into the arms of death and saved his master Claudio. The love and self-sacrifice of animals for human beings was simply admirable.

He thought that his journey was a bit of a mixed bag, much like his life, as his chief editor' had already pointed out to him.

He remembered his first snow classes near Grenoble, that would be his next appointment.

The Pelletier family was in the midst of preparing to pack their bags and enjoy their son Julien's few days of winter vacation.

Their small apartment in eastern Paris was in turmoil.

Maurice and Jacqueline, the parents, were in full swing, because something was always missing when they arrived.

Once it was the son's forgotten skis, another time the papers of the Renault Scenic, they had noticed it during a police control in Vizille on the N85, they had been obliged to return to Paris, to present them to the police station of Grenoble, with the litany of reproaches from his wife Jacqueline all along the way.

Every year around the fifteenth of February, it was like a pilgrimage, he rented a two-room apartment in the winter sports resort *"Les Deux Alpes"* in Isère.

The Alpes de Mont-de-Lans was more than three thousand six hundred meters high, and on the top of the glacier you could ski in summer thanks to the eternal snow.

Ideal for beginners, but also reserved for experienced sliders like Maurice and Jacqueline who enjoyed slaloming in the powder and doing off-piste skiing between the fir trees. The resort with its one hundred and twenty kilometers of slopes delighted skiers of all categories.

This year Julien had celebrated his thirteenth birthday and the year before he had brilliantly passed his third star at the ESF[12].

The six hundred kilometers of highway between Paris and the Isère department had been swallowed in no time by the Scenic. A short lunch stop at the Courtepaille in Lyon-La Part Dieu, warmed the hearts and cooled the car, said Maurice; they were ready to attack the mountain.

They had passed Grenoble, Vizille, the Bourg d'Oisans and after a passage along the Vénon at nine hundred meters of altitude, they were going to start the seven kilometers of ascent, nicknamed the vertical of the devil, with their Renault.

They crossed the alleys of the village of Venosc, wrapped in its winter coat.

---

[12] French Skiing School

Halfway up, they left the Lake of Chambon dam on their left. This was the place they were waiting for to start their favorite song:

"Come on, driver, come on driver, come on That quickly became":

— Faster driver, faster driver, faster!

As the evening wore on, Maurice pointed to the peaks, their snow glistening in the setting sun.

Julien marveled to see the lights of the chalets at the bottom of the valley making phantasmagorical figures on the white slopes.

The slopes were covered with snow but the road was clear, on the left side a vertiginous precipice plunged towards fir trees weighed down by the snow.

On the right side, waterfalls of bluish ice and their suspended stalagmites glittered with a thousand lights.

The arrival at the resort of "Les Deux Alpes" left them stunned as usual. The chalets and hotels were decked out in their best colors, a smell of ozone wafted through the air from who knows where, the clatter of heavy ski boots echoed on the asphalt road, a light wind blew, making the cables of the ski lifts tinkle; for sure they had reached their destination.

They parked in front of the Edelweiss hotel to say hello to Mrs. Bale, the owner, and went back to the *"les Myosotis"* building to settle in their residence.

Tomorrow would be another day, with the taking of the ski passes in the House of the Union of Initiative and the consultation of the weather forecast to come.

Maurice and Jacqueline had decided that Julien would go with them off-road. Now he was doing a great job *(The practice of parallel skiing)* wonderfully and the kid made them proud.

Maurice provided everyone with safety equipment, parabolic skis, a Trekking backpack, a helmet, anti-reflection glasses, an anti-sunburn stick, a sunburn ointment, an ARVA[13], a bottle of water, a sandwich for a snack.

Earlier in the afternoon, a team of trackers was on the slopes of the Écrins massif at the top of the Meije at nearly four thousand meters, nicknamed the roof of the Deux Alpes:

— Is everyone at his position?

— Let's go, guys, announced José Alvares, mountain climber and rescue worker, and also the site's operational manager, into his walkie-talkie.

Five people were spread out on the snowy slopes. Each one had a precise task, to do some coring in order to know the risks of avalanches for the days to come.

The operation consisted in pushing a tube into the snow cover, bringing out a cylinder of ice of about 50 centimeters which allowed to read the different superimposed layers.

---

[13] Avalanche rescue device

A first deep icy layer, on which a second finer granular layer that could be used as a ball bearing and a third layer that fell last night that rolled on the second one and ended up as an avalanche slab, taking everything on its way.

They stored their ice cylinders in a refrigerated compartment of their motoski and headed back down to the valley for examination.

Their mission was not over, they had to set off mini-avalanches from the Grave mountain and the Pied Moutet-Vallée Blanche area.

They threw firecrackers in strategic places, and the snow slabs broke off by themselves with the explosion, rolling down the slope in a roar and a fog of snow.

Many skiers liked to go off-piste, the descents in the *"wilderness"*, evolving between the fir trees, were their hobby. The valleys of the Meije were accessible from La Grave, but they were often unaware of the dangers of the mountain and had to be constantly reminded of them.

In the heart of the resort, at the café *"Les Marmottes"*, a meeting was held between mountain rescue workers.

José Alvares, the leader, dressed in the red of the ESF instructors uniform, was standing and began his preamble by weighing his words

— As you know, tomorrow it will be sunny. These last days it has been snowing a lot. The different thicknesses of the snow strata indicate a high probability of avalanche.

The groomers[14] have smoothed the marked trails, but we will have to be on the lookout for off-road enthusiasts.

A tall man stood up in turn:

— My men and their dogs are ready to help you, said Roger Krazinsky, the head of the canine rescue team.

— Thanks Roger, I know I can rely on your brigade. Your two German Shepherds and your Labrador have already done wonders in searching for buried skiers.

— Yes José, it's a matter of speed and flair. The pleasures of the mountains are sometimes dangerous. Under several meters of snow, victims need quick help.

— Only rescue dogs are able to react quickly and find them thanks to their sense of smell.

Our professionalism is recognized by two types of official structures, the Army and the Police force, in partnership with the winter sports resorts.

Currently our offices are located in Grenoble, and only ANENA, the National Association for the Study of Snow and Avalanches, is authorized to train certified dogs!

Philippe Labarre, dog handler, as every morning, went out of his chalet to bring the food to his little pets in the kennel next to his property in Vizilloise. He raised several German Shepherd dogs for rescue and protection.

---

[14] Tracked vehicle to flatten snowy trails

His favorite, Olga, had a good record of success, with several rescues to her credit.

She was an avalanche dog but also a search dog for survivors of collapses like the Morandi bridge in Genoa, where she found several children trapped in a toy store.

Olga had given birth to several puppies that had found a buyer quickly. Only one female remained in her bed and she did not want to leave it. The puppy followed her everywhere, even during the training sessions that had started again.

The ball of hair had a white patch under the chest and Philippe named her *"Neige"*, she would be perfect to follow in her mother's footsteps. Like all German Shepherd puppies, Neige had silky curly hair that would later become erin.

Her clumsy demeanor would soon become a queenly bearing, as Olga took to sniffing out the scents of people buried under rock or snow.

In Vizille, Philippe and his kennel were known as the white wolf, and the winter period became his favorite season.

"Always ready to help your fellow man" was his motto.

The Pelletier family had just had breakfast and was ready to hit the slopes. Maurice double-checked the equipment, especially the ARVA, the avalanche tracking devices.

They took the Jandri express which took them in a few minutes to the foot of the glacier, to the Dôme du Puy Salié at 3421 meters. Perfect for a gradual resumption of sculling in powder snow.

The three of them set off down the side of the mountain still untouched by ski tracks.

They stopped on the top of a bump to admire the magnificent panorama of the Meije and the Mont-Blanc sparkling with their snowy cap.

— After having seen that, we can die quietly, exclaimed Maurice! Come on, let's go, if we want to be able to offer ourselves a glass of mulled wine at the high altitude restaurant *"La patache."*

They set off again in a straight line across the slope, the wind from the speed preventing them from hearing the dull roar emanating from their summit. A patch of snow broke off over their heads, rolling down the mountain in a swirl of snow and fog, carrying them away.

<>

A bell rang in the premises of the Gendarmerie in the village of Les Deux Alpes. Major Jérôme Tiercelin knew this bell, it was an avalanche alert. He took his binoculars to identify the area where the slide had started. He recognized the Dome du Puy Saliè from where a cloud of snow was emanating, recognizable as an avalanche in progress.

He called in direct line the mountain rescuers, who themselves will warn their colleagues, with their dogs specialized in the civil search.

Already about fifty people with their long poles were present in front of the premises. It was necessary to make quickly, human lives were in danger.

The intervention platoon had left a while ago, and put the helicopter on standby, which might be needed to descend into the valley to the hospital in Grenoble.

<>

Maurice emerged from behind a fir tree that had protected him from the snow flow. He looked at the flow that had just swept them away, it was a hundred meters wide and five - six hundred meters long from the summit.

He had been extremely lucky to be protected by this resinous. Unfortunately he was alone with all this snow piled up. He called his wife and child, without success. A deadly silence reigned on the spot.

He was in a valley and at the top some skiers were waving. He fell to his knees:
— Help, help, help, he cried and stammered.

Big snowmobiles with three people on board, holding long poles, were coming from everywhere.
— Hurry, my wife and kid are buried somewhere under this snow. They are equipped with avalanche transceivers, hurry!

The phone rang at Philippe Labane's house, a mournful music that he had pre-recorded and that meant that his services would be needed.
— Olga, Neige, come on my beauties, let's not keep waiting those who are asking for us.

They arrived on the area a few minutes later, thanks to the helicopter of the gendarmes.

It was a couple and their son who were off-piste; with the ARVA, finding them should be easy.

The father was protected by a tree and was safe, the wife was also safe, only the boy was still missing.

An hour and a half had passed and the young man's chances of survival were diminishing by the minute.

If the burial lasts less than 18 minutes, survival is estimated at 90%. Between 18 and 35 minutes, it drops to 34%. It is still 20% up to 120 minutes and only 7% after 130 minutes.

To hear Maurice and his wife Jacqueline screaming the name of their son Julien at the top of their lungs gave the rescuers on the spot a boost. At each syllable of the name Philippe's hair stood on its head.

He didn't understand why his dog Olga, accompanied by her puppy Neige, wanted to search outside the avalanche area. He decided to follow the instincts of his German Shepherds.

Apparently the boy's ARVA was not working, it had been almost two hours since the deadline passed, how was he going to find Julien?

Neige suddenly began to scrape the snow, followed by his mother Olga. Philippe alerted the other rescuers, who all arrived with their shovels and pulled the boy out. He was purple and unconscious, in cardiorespiratory arrest.

Julien was placed on a stretcher and the helicopter flew to the emergency room of the Grenoble-Alpes University Hospital.

In a coma, the doctors warmed his body, his temperature had dropped below 25°.

Maurice and Jacqueline, the parents, were crying like crazy in front of their son's bed.

Even Philippe's eyes were shining, the whining of the little dog Neige was distressing.

The emergency doctors specified that it would take a miracle to bring him back to life and that the next few hours would be decisive.

The chapel of the hospital was full to bursting, as often after this kind of disaster, even the people of Grenoble came to pray and meditate.

Back in his chalet in Vizille, Philippe was still overwhelmed with emotion. Julien the young boy did not deserve to perish like that. He went in to take a shower and left to clear his head in front of his TV, which he put on mute.

There was a commotion in his kennel, he went out to see what was going on, the dogs were howling to death and spinning around in their cages in panic.

Neige was biting the fence as if she wanted to escape from her pen. He went to open the door for her and she licked between her legs, what did she want?

He joined her in front of her 4WD, what did she want?

— What do you want, Neige, to see Julien again, the one you practically rescued? Well, you are right, I too want to know what happens to him.

The twenty kilometers separating Vizille from Grenoble were swallowed in about thirty minutes.

Maurice and Jacqueline were drinking coffee in front of Julien's room when they saw the little dog Neige scratching at his door.

— What's going on, said Maurice when he saw Philippe?

— Neige made a hell of a fuss back at the kennel, as if she wanted to see Julien again, dogs have an instinct for self-preservation and often perceive events that we do not control.

— Yes, but Julien is still in a coma.

— Let's let her in and follow her, he said.

Neige jumped on the bed and nibbled on the boy's earlobes, and he shivered under the sheets and opened his eyes.

— It's you Neige, I had you in my dreams, you prevented me from sinking when I was under the ice.

Mom, dad, he said this little dog spoke to me when I was at my wits' end, she is my guardian angel, she advised me to be patient and told me to adopt her.

Maurice, Jacqueline and Philippe were in tears in front of this charming picture, Neige licking her new master with all her tongue.

Chapter VI
Yuna, the Persian She-cat

Alex knew about mountain rescue dogs, but it's impossible to know when they were first rescued, probably before the nineteenth century, according to some sources.

As is often the case, history revolves around myths.

In this case, it was Barry, a St. Bernard who lived in the last century, who filled this role. He gained notoriety by saving four lost pilgrims from a blizzard.

After his death he was embalmed and preserved in the natural history museum in Bern.

The little dog Neige will now discover her new family.

After laying out his map of France, Alex closed his eyes and let his finger choose his next destination, the "Finistère".

— What does all this mean, began Martine Piccinel, director of the Douarnenez retirement home?

You are announcing a new rebellion of the staff, to go on strike while we are starting the accounting of the establishment, it is a shame.

Everyone knows about my difficulties with the board of directors, and they're pushing my head under the water at a time when the accounts are in the red.

Do they want me dead or what?

Anaëlle Lebreton, her assistant, tried to console her boss.

— Keep your cool, boss. It's just a blip, when you get the grants from the ministry, you'll be back on track.

<>

Further up in the Finistère department, in Kerlaz, Kilian Lebrac lived with his mother Eloane in a small house, at the bottom of a small garden, a few minutes from the Crozon peninsula. A Persian she-cat, with an immaculate white dress named Yuna completed the picture. It was Eloane's favorite animal and she was her pride and joy in animal beauty contests.

She had won many of them.

Kilian's father had died of a long and painful cancer and Eloane had put all her love into her beloved son.

He had moved her to the second floor of his house, where she was perfectly independent.

But for some time now, Eloane had been absent. In addition, she felt watched and followed when she went to the village butcher. This form of persecution finally alerted Kilian, who made an appointment with the doctor for more information.

The diagnosis came down on a Thursday; your mother is suffering from the onset of Alzheimer's. You will have to give her all your love.

The days passed with their share of ups and downs. The neighborhood had been warned and everyone was pulling together. The Bretons are known for their rebellious side but also for their patience.

They helped Kilian as best they could, when he went to work, and the neighbors looked after Eloane's mother.

Sometimes he would rush back to his mother's house, lost and completely naked in the middle of a crossroads.

Kilian owned a computer store in the beautiful town of Douarnenez, near the tip of Penmarc'h. The five kilometers to his home were swallowed in a few minutes and allowed him to keep an eye on his mother's outbursts.

As an only son, he became the caregiver of a dependent mother. Being his own boss, the social organizations provided him with the minimum assistance.

When he went to knock on the door of the social worker in his village, he was met with one disappointment after another. Yes, he was entitled to at least the APA[15], an aid provided by the General Council of the Department.

Home care was billed at full price, due to his high tax returns, and the fact that he had exceeded the income limit for family allowances prevented him from receiving any assistance from the State.

---

[15] Personalized Autonomy Aid.

Many voices were raised in her family urging her to take early retirement in order to take care of her mother full time.

How to make them understand that taking care of an Alzheimer's patient was not something that could be done at the drop of a hat and during a few hours a day. Constant 24-hours care was necessary and mandatory.

A person with this disease was like oil on the fire, ready to start any fire accidentally. She could leave the milk on the gas, or the water running from the overflowing tub.

Only Yuna earned her indulgence and got petted willy-nilly, without impatience.

A cat flap had been installed on the front door to allow the cat to move around the house and garden.

From time to time, Éloane would leave for her lost world, at these moments Kilian could not reach her, she looked at him with inexpressive and lifeless eyes, he realized that all his filial love had vanished forever, even Yuna guessing the uneasiness made herself small and hid in a corner.

In rage and despair, he broke down in torrents of tears, burning and useless. It was the disease that was expressing itself.

Yuna would go and hide under the bed, not understanding the punches in the walls that Kilian would throw in fits of anger and frustration.

A service provider provided her with care and cleaning ladies, and the city council gave her meals on wheels.

Each day, a first person from the town hall brought her lunch and dinner in trays, a second one came to get her up, wash her and make her eat breakfast. At the end of the morning, a third person brought the first Ebixa medication and prepared her meal.

In the afternoon, a fourth person made her take her second medication, Reminyl, and in the evening, the fifth person made her take a bath, a light meal and put her to bed.

This went on for a whole year, and it took a toll on her meager finances.

Fortunately, her doctor, Dr. Arén, had her hospitalized for two or three weeks at the Hospital Center Laennec near her pavilion, just enough time for Kilian to rest.

Sometimes she would have sudden bursts of anger and become a real fury, destroying everything in her path: plates, torn clothes, broken chairs. This small, good-looking woman would turn into King Kong.

At the Hospital, he was advised to call the ambulance, the firemen and the police during his spats.

So many useless words, because the Police do not come to the hospital for family quarrels!

So Kilian went to try to file a complaint against his mother:

— How dare you do that, a policewoman told him.

We do not receive this kind of complaint, go figure: a son against his mother! You can only make a hand-rail for this type of event!

One evening, when Éloane was asking for her driver's license for the umpteenth time, even though Kilian had already given it back to her and she had lost it, she became furious

— I want my papers, you hide them from me, give them to me right now.

— Mom, I've already given them to you. We'll talk about it tomorrow if you like.

Kilian had learned to defuse explosive situations, leaving her to calm down alone.

He went to bed, keeping an attentive ear on what was happening above his head. Not a sound, she had gone to bed too.

The next day, he was awakened by a loud noise, his door was hit by a heavy object.

— My papers, right now! cried his mother, hitting the door frame with a massive hammer.

A neighbor in her adjoining garden got involved:

— Éloane, the police will arrive, I called them!

— Damn Huguette, you're against me too!

Kilian, on his way out, tried to calm the swelling gust of wind:

— Mom, be nice, calm down.

Éloane took her slipper and hit her son;

— Shut up, I don't know you, leave me alone!

A police car stopped in front of the house, two officials got out and started a conversation:

— Hello Mrs. Lebrac, why all the commotion?

At the sight of the uniforms, Éloane, relented and replied:

— Hello, I don't understand why you came here.

— Listen, Mrs. Lebrac, your son filed a report with the police at the police station a few days ago.

Go to the hospital and get yourself checked out so we can be sure you're okay.

After much procrastination, and seeing that all this talk was not bearing fruit, the officer got angry:

— We've been talking for almost an hour and a half, if you don't make up your mind, I'll send an ambulance to take you away, willingly or not!

So, Éloane went upstairs to lock herself in her house!

— Kilian, paramedics are coming, I advise you not to intervene or watch, it will be painful for you both!

A hospital van pulled up in front of the entrance with a screech of tires, and Kilian heard heavy footsteps coming up the stairs.

The paramedics broke down the door and cleared away the furniture that Éloane had piled up in front of it:

— Kilian, my son, help, help!

Kilian cried and punched the wall in fury at Alzheimer's and the world.

After spending the night consoling Yuna, who was shaking all over like she did every time Eloane was hospitalized, Kilian went to the emergency room to find her.

When he entered her room, a second woman was bedridden like her mother, but she was naked as a worm on her bed, the sheets pushed back and piled up on the floor, the night must have been agitated!

Kilian passed straight as an I, avoiding looking at the nudity exposed to the eyes. His mother was reassured and a little drugged by the drugs, smiled weakly at him:

— My love, did you come? Come and give me a kiss!

As if the memories of the previous day had gone and disappeared from her memory.

She was back to being the sweet, charming little girl who called him on the phone to wish him a good day at work. Unfortunately, she went back to sleep and left for unexplored lands.

Kilian went out again without looking at the other woman who hailed him:

— Sir, sir, my husband is coming to get me, can you call him on the phone?

Kilian pulled up the sheets and covered the old woman, who was clearly not in her right mind.

— Madam, you have a call bulb to ring the nurses, he said, pointing to the utensil hanging from a wire. She took it in hand, brought it to her mouth and said:

— Hello, hello, is anyone there?

Nearly choking with laughter, Kilian called a care girl and explained the situation.

— Don't worry, she said, this is the Alzheimer unit, I'll take care of it.

Kilian went to the police station in Quimper to thank the officials who had prevented his mother's outbursts.

He met the policewoman who had accompanied the officer the previous days:

— Ah, I recognize you, she said, you are the son of Éloane the Alzheimer. Your mother left the mark of her teeth on my shoulder, she was unchained in the ambulance. What a little piece of woman!

Kilian reflected on the absurdity of life. His mother was approaching eighty and did not deserve to be forgotten by her family. His cousins, the daughters of his mother's three sisters, had been very angry with him since the beginning of his Alzheimer's disease.

The reproaches had been made, the criticisms had followed and then the angers against this son who did not want to listen to reason and who stubbornly wanted to separate himself from the author of his Days.

But how to make them understand this disease that confuses people and makes them forget the immediate memories, those that make you go back to your steps, without knowing what you had to do, the reminiscence of the tools you used to use and that remain in your hands, without possibility of control.

For a theater actor, the missing word of a phrase learned and recited thousands of times. For a surgeon, his scalpel raised on the body of a patient, whose brilliance frightens him and whose action stuns him.

The news was not good, the head doctor of the geriatric service took him aside:

— You will not always be able to take care of your mother, the moment she confuses day and night, it will be hellish for you. Let the right people take care of her and look after her.

Indeed, a few days later in the night, Kilian heard a loud noise overhead. He went upstairs to the newsroom and found his mother in the dark, ass over head in the chairs in her living room.

— Kilian, help, I can't find the light, stammered Éloane.

— But Mom, the switches are near your head.

More fear than harm, he lifted her up and put her back to bed. He was about to leave when his mother held him by the arm:

— I'm afraid, don't leave me alone in this big house!

This scene continued day after day, with Kilian looking after his mother at night and working hard during the day.

Finally, she slept peacefully during the day and was active at night, without worrying about her son's health.

Life was becoming unbearable for Kilian, his store was deserted by his customers, finances were falling and a solution had to be found quickly.

Yuna the little she-cat was waiting for Eloane's naps to purr on her lap. She ignored her mistress's angry outbursts and forgave her all her extravagances. She walked her majestic way through the house, and disappeared at Eloane's mood swings.

Kilian had noticed that his mother was looking into the emerald green eyes of the Persian cat and that it was comforting.

The time had come to find a home for her that specialized in Alzheimer's. How would the cat behave when she no longer saw her mistress? She would only eat when Éloane was near her, and would disdainfully pass by the bowl Kilian was preparing for her.

She chose an EHPAD with the sweet name of Jardins Clos in Douarnenez. Benefiting from the ASH *(Social Aid for Accommodation)* the daily rates were reasonable. A place was going to become available following the death of a resident, it was unfortunately an obligatory wait, the elderly and dependent people increased in an exponential way these last times!

One of the prerogatives requested was a weekly visit from Yuna.

The director of the facility, Martine Piccinel, practiced pet therapy, and felt that pets significantly calmed the residents. She agreed to Kilian's request and perhaps Yuna would find a four-legged friend at the EHPAD.

A week passed, then two. Kilian took advantage of the visits to his clients' homes to drop by and see his mother several times a day. She couldn't bear to see him go and it was one crying fit after another.

Doctor Dubarron of the institution asked him to come and see his mother once or twice a week, which was more than enough and would not affect his mental state.

Weeks, months, years passed, three Christmases followed each other with their processions of gifts and snow, spreading a beneficial blanket over the EHPAD.

Yuna walked royally between the Alzheimer's wearing a magnificent bow, wrapped in ruby. She dodged the caresses in a skilful way, without offending anyone.

Eloane spent most of her time dozing in her wheelchair, so Yuna would come over and rub her face with the hand that was dangling, then with a soft leap would sit on her lap and purr.

Approaching eighty-six, Eloane had lost the ability to speak for two years and was only intermittently feeding, refusing to eat anything.

At times, Kilian would feed her with fruit yoghurt, a delicacy she had loved when her life had run on straight lines, without constraints or arbitrariness.

Now he selflessly surrounded his mother with all his love, wiping her mouth when she drooled and rejected her food, straightening her body and pulling up her pillow, for better comfort.

She wasn't eating much anymore and had lost almost a fifth of her original weight.

As he became concerned, Dr. Dubarron told him that Éloane was no longer eating and that this circumstance would soon mark the end of her existence.

He continued his explanation:
— Alzheimer's disease results from a slow degeneration of neurons, starting in the hippocampus *(a brain structure essential for memory)* and then spreading to the rest of the brain. It is

characterized by disorders of recent memory, executive functions, and orientation in time and space. The patient progressively loses his cognitive faculties and his autonomy.

Our brain sends orders to the different members and organs of our body to move, walk, open our mouths, eat, swallow and breathe.

Imagine Kilian, that the signal emitted by this one is not done any more, that you *"forget"* to breathe, that your lungs do not make any more their job of aerator, that your heart *"forgets"* to beat... it is what will happen with Éloane!

—What more can I do to love my mom or help her in her last moments, Kilian begged with tears in his eyes?

—Your mom's subconscious is awake, but that's what we men of science think. I think that somewhere inside her she hears you and understands you. Continue to take care of her, it's the best thing you can do right now!

Every evening, when he went back to his house in Kerlaz, Yuna the Persian meowed to split the soul. Without a doubt, she sensed that the end of her mistress was near.

Kilian tried with all his strength to avoid tears in front of the she-cat, she had scratched her several times when he was crying out; it seemed to say, it's my turn to be sad and to whine, not yours!

One evening when he was about to leave, Doctor Dubarron came to see him with a serious look.

— My friend, your mom has come to the end, in a day or two, you must expect to see her make her last journey!

All this is sad and painful, but I believe that her way of the cross will end peacefully, thanks to your love and devotion.

Many of our residents die alone and without a loved one at their bedside.

And I must tell you that our entire hospital department is proud to have known both of you.

The next day, while in Éloane's room, the doctors were taking notes and the nurses were giving her morning care.

Through the windows a bright February sun was trying to break through the haze outside.

It had been a long night, and Yuna had been raging against the curtains and furniture, and had torn Kilian's bed to shreds, as if blaming him for his mistress's near departure. He was too unhappy and had let her do it. His fur had withered and his body was flayed from not eating, this little animal was suffering from Éloane's illness.

Doctor Dubarron came to see him:

— I just examined your mother, her heart is beating weakly, I think she is resisting and does not want to leave without your permission. Go see her one last time!

Kilian approached the bed, which seemed smaller than usual. His mother's breathing was coming in fits and starts. He stroked her snowy hair, and his mother seemed to wake up to his touch.

She opened her eyes and looked at him, the same way she used to look at him, full of love and tenderness in her eyes, in a breath she whispered:

— Kilian... my lovely darling

And she died in his arms, a slight smile floating on her lips!

Chapter VII
Hatchi, the Akita Inu dog

It is often said that when we are ready to die, we look back on our lives. Alex hoped that Éloane would have been able to see the love of his son Kilian before the big departure.

Brittany was moving away, now his next region was "Normandie", land of cheese and good food. The Ibis hotel in the center of Rouen near the Cathedral was perfect for his next editorial.

The CISMF laboratory of the "Normandie region" was ringing with the hooting of fire sirens, the flashing lights on the roof were sparkling.

The Rouen Fire and Rescue Center had been alerted and was on its way, all their horns blaring.

The fire had started in the west wing where the labs were conducting animal experiments.

The cages containing monkeys, cats, dogs and other residents were in the east wing, a little further away.

Everything had been designed at night by the firebombers, while the animals and researchers were not on site, each one was resting in their cages and in their beds.

The association Anima Save announced its exuberance by dazzling actions, but without endangering the animals and the people.

Their leitmotiv: to show the reality in the slaughterhouses, the mistreatment of the animals, the maintenance of the premises which leaves something to be desired and the products which can become unfit for consumption, these factories of death are their first objectives.

This is what we see in the images unveiled by Anima Save, denouncing the conditions of breeding of laying hens. They appear deplumed, living in an environment invaded by lice, maggots. The ground is strewn with poultry corpses in a state of decomposition.

The association had decided to focus on the research and animal experimentation laboratories because before the death in the slaughterhouses, it was not better in the labs that martyred the animals by sticking electrodes and all sorts of microbial dirt in their bodies.

The soldiers of the association, as they were called, did not hide and signed their crimes with large tags on the walls *"Stop the death camps"*.

This time they decided to open the cages of the guinea pigs, causing a joyful uproar in the east wing lab.

The alarms had been turned off and the monkeys were swinging on suspended neon lights, some with electrodes still stuck in their craniums. The dogs were chasing the cats around, running and jumping in every corner.

One madman had the unfortunate idea to open the glass door of the lab and the animals scattered in the large corridors towards the exit of the establishment.

The leader of the commando, Audrey Corroy, stimulated the group's ardor:

— Gentlemen, don't be reasonable and show these murderers our motives!

She asked about a row of metal chairs, the meaning of which she knew. The rhesus macaques were immobilized in these instruments of torture where their limbs and necks were locked.

Their brains were connected directly to measuring devices; these very impressive devices are called *"work chairs."* They are used to channel the movements of the monkeys, and to prevent them from hurting themselves by moving, and especially from disturbing the instruments by touching the wires and electrodes.

The scientific community does not like to show the experiments performed on these guinea pigs, for fear of offending sensitive souls!

She approached all the cells to check their contents, a frightened puppy was huddled in the bottom of a kennel. When she passed in front of the little dog, he rushed into her arms, squealing.

— Well, what are you doing here, little rascal, she said.

Some puppies had not been tattooed by their owners and had just arrived on the spot.

A label placed on the cage indicated the origin, the date of entry and also the date of exit which often expressed the death of the animal.

It was an Akita Inu, short-haired type, coming from Japan, of large size at the adult size, with a round head shape, of female sex. Her white coat made her look like a small polar bear from Antarctica.

For the time being, this little ball of hair seemed to have adopted Audrey, and did not want to leave her arms.

Excited, she knew the risk she was taking in removing the animal. Was it reasonable, she thought?

Her choice was quickly made, she stole the tag and placed a blank one in its place. Since the Akita was not listed, there was a chance that its disappearance would go unnoticed.

The lab was now silent, only a few mice were running along the baseboards, weighed down by growths on their bodies, no doubt from diseases inoculated by the researchers.

The next morning, a headline appeared on the front page of the Actu-Normandie newspaper: *"CISMF laboratory vandalized and emptied of its guinea pigs"*.

The general manager of the lab, Germain MacMillan, cried out in horror and did not take off:

— What is this souk, it is still the assoc' Anima Save which is at the origin of the depredations!

— Yes chief answered the assistant Sophia Marlin, and I filled you the deposit of complaint to the Gendarmerie of Rouen.

— Listen Sophia, we must not make any commotion. Currently, public opinion is against animal abuse and other genetic manipulations. We have to play it low profile, without making a fuss. The Minister of Health has just rang the bell, reminding me to *"not make any noise"*.

The last European elections put the ecologists in third position, it would not be a question of displeasing the power in place and to see our subsidies decreased or stopped.

So alert our maintenance and research department to find the animals that are still in the wild. Particularly the rhesus macaques which must be happy in the trees of the nearby forest.

<>

Audrey Corroy was feverishly perusing the day's newspaper. The fire had been eradicated, supposedly quickly, by the firemen and in the East wing, the main cages had found their fellow creatures. There was no trace of her Anima Save association, the tags had been erased, a blanket of silence seemed to have spread over the place. She didn't know if she should be happy about it or complain about it.

No legal action had been taken, no doubt President MacMillan had something to do with it.

Audrey turned around and saw her puppy staring at her and wagging his little tail frantically!

— What am I going to call you, scoundrel?

We saved you from the evil clutches of the lab, a name of rescue would suit you, no?

Well, I choose Hatchi, which reminds me of that wonderful movie with Richard Gere. Judging by your positive head nod, you must like it. Come on my dear, let's get to know your new

94

home. You'll be able to familiarize yourself with my two children Philippe and Marie when they come back from school.

<>

The bell for the end of classes had just rung at the Molière elementary school in Elbeuf. Marie and Philippe, 10 and 12 years old, got dressed and went out the main door.

Today Philippe had to take care of his little sister because Audrey couldn't pick them up. He took Mary by the hand and ran down the road to the bus stop.

Jeanna Figlio was driving her Mercedes briskly, her job as a lawyer didn't leave her much time to enjoy herself, she had just written her last notes on the dictaphone and slowed down as she approached the public school on Rue du Tapis Vert.

She suddenly received a huge punch in her chest, her vision blurred and she lost consciousness, the uncontrolled Mercedes mowed down the two kids in its race and ended in the bus stop.

<>

Audrey was cooking pancakes under the eyes of the puppy, this one was making jumps of goat and rubbing in the legs of his new mistress:

— Stop it Hatchi, you too will get your pancake, be patient! Your little masters will soon discover you, I can't wait to see their reels when they see you.

The ringing of the landline phone resounded mournfully in the dining room, Audrey's eyebrows furrowed as she looked at

Hatchi, the little dog had laid her ears back as if she sensed what was going to happen:

— Hello, yes it's me! What's going on, Madam Principal? NOOO, I'M COMING!

<>

The emergency room of the Intercommunal Hospital of Elbeuf-Louviers-Val-de-Reuil was informed that two children had been hit by a car, that an ambulance was on its way and that everything was prepared for a delicate intervention!

Two fire trucks were escorting the rescue vehicle, when it entered the dedicated area. One firefighter came out with tears in his eyes:

—The little girl is in a coma but she will recover. According to the witnesses, the kid saw the car running towards them, he had time to push and move his little sister out of the way and took the car head-on. He died.

A Suzuki 4WD drove up behind them in a hurry. Audrey, disheveled and livid, got out like a madwoman:

— Where are my kids?

A firefighter gently took her arm to escort her into the premises.

— Come on, Madam, I'll show you the way, we've just arrived.

When he told her that her son had died, Audrey screamed like a wounded beast, which made the fireman and the nurses shiver. He also told her that the person driving the Mercedes had also died of a massive heart attack just before hitting the children. Witnesses saw her collapsed on her steering wheel at the moment of impact.

Several weeks later, Marie was still in bed at the University Hospital of Saint-Aubin-lès-Elbeuf. The sacrifice of her older brother had deeply affected her and her legs were as if paralyzed:

— It is a psychosomatic condition, explained Dr. Samuel Karma, head of the psychiatric department. When the mind uses the body to express itself, the body somatizes.

It is a real disease, in which emotional factors, anxiety, depression or shocks *(especially mourning)* can affect an organ and in this case it is your child's legs.

I believe that you live alone with your children, I advise you to find a third person or an animal to make your little girl aware of the joys of life again.

— Yes doctor, I just adopted a puppy, which I haven't shown to Marie yet, do you think his presence will be beneficial?

— Absolutely, it's a happy coincidence, if I may say so! Marie has to go out at the end of the week, come and pick her up in her wheelchair, you have to get her out of her torpor. Don't show the puppy too quickly, let it get used to it. After two or three days, you will be able to make the introductions.

Audrey entered the room pushing a wheelchair:

— Hello my beloved, it's your day out, you're back home, I've made you some pancakes as you like them.

— Mom, I'm so comfortable here, I've even managed to make friends in the department and with the patients

— Marie, you have to go back to school and your friends at home are waiting for you too. Anyway, you can come back here for the check-up in a few days.

— Mom, I'm afraid I'm going to find memories of my brother, she said with a tear.

— My beloved, your brother is in the stars watching over us, you know how I feel about that. There are fantastic forces around us, and we never quite disappear. Dad left after a long illness, and told us that sooner or later we would join him. I think that both father and son go fishing as they did on land.
You don't have to worry about Philip, he is close to you as he was on the day of the accident.
And they both cried their eyes out.

In accordance with Professor Karma's instructions, Audrey had locked Hatchi in a small storage room, waiting to be introduced to Mary.

They entered the house, with Audrey pushing Marie. Little notes were taped everywhere:

"Happy homecoming, Marie."

— Mom, I love you!

A squeak was heard, followed by a frantic run across the tile floor:

— Mom, what's that noise?

— I wanted to surprise you these days, but a little friend doesn't seem to have the patience to wait. I'm going to open the storeroom door for it before it breaks it down.

A white rocket came out of the closet, jumped on Marie's lap and licked her face.

"Mom, how did you guess that I wanted a little dog, it is quite adorable, thank you Mam."

Audrey felt the tears invade her eyes, her daughter had called her "Mam" as in the time when their life was beautiful and without clouds.

Nota Bene : Hatchi the Akita Inn dog, film in 2009 directed by Lasse Hallström with Richard Gère, shows the whole character of the animal, it is him who chooses his master and not the opposite. He will be faithful to him until his death.

Malcom Akita Inn dog, infuenceur to 765 000 subscribers well known on the Instagram network.

Chapter VIII
Syrius, the German Shepherd

Speciesists and other vegans define the animal as equal to the human being, are they right?

In any case, the Hatchi puppy will participate in the recomposition of this fragmented family.

Christophe the head editor has just called me, the military accept my investigation on animals in the army, and offer me a permanent entry.

I will be able to put down my *"gear"*, excuse my suitcases, in the camp of Mourmelon, the Mecca of soldierly exercises in France.

<>

"Here is the military camp of Chalon which was inaugurated in 1857 by Napoleon III, and had a great importance during the Second Empire".

The demonstration of Lieutenant Colonel Pallanco Juan was intended to train the two thousand soldiers who came from all over the world for a strategic training on the camp of Mourmelon in the Marne.

"Citadel Guilbert 2018" was the name of the exercise of the last weeks on the camp of Mourmelon-le-Grand.

The soldiers from fourteen different nationalities had the objective to learn to coordinate and work together.

For this exercise, the six thousand square meters of the military camp were occupied by the troops. Canvas tents as far as the eye could see, sixty-five in all, but also one hundred and sixty shelters *(modular shelters)* to house the command posts.

The dog battalion belonging to the 132nd regiment was part of the movement and had set up their fifty or so men and as many dogs in Section 5.

Colonel Edouard commanding officer of the 132nd BCAT recalled that the first award given to a dog was by Napoleon himself in the XIXth century.

More recently, Fitas was awarded the National Defense Gold Medal with Silver Star. Captured during an operation in Afghanistan, he was held hostage for four months. *This is to say that military dogs are rewarded in the same way as their masters."*

The team leader and dog handler Joan Capdeveme was a warrant officer and knew his specialty, to train and educate his dog Syrius in order to use its sensory and behavioral qualities in the framework of the allocated missions, protection of sensitive installations, combat support, especially in external operations, search for explosives and drugs.

Under his command, he had known six dogs which each time made him a perfect ally. His seventh *"partner"*, a German Shepherd dog, lived in the kennel of his bunker, with other four-legged companions. Syrius had just turned four years old and was able to leap three meters without a run-up to intercept a hostile individual. He was in the prime of his life, unlike Joan, his handler, who had passed the forty-year mark and was ready for a well-deserved retirement.

His reconversion was assured as a security dog agent for the private sector.

When he retired, he would take his dog, who lived in perfect symbiosis with him.

Syrius obeyed Joan's every word, and they had a last mission in the Central African Republic.

<>

In December 2013, the Epervier force, based in Chad, provided a C130 Hercules, a CASA CN 235 and their crews, to provide an air bridge between Libreville in Gabon, and Bangui in the Central African Republic, as part of the reinforcement of the Sangaris force.

This is the seventh French military intervention since the country's independence in 1960.

After crossing France-Africa in the McDonnell Douglas C17 troop carrier, Joan Capdeverne, accompanied by Syrius, returned to his unit based in M'Poko ready for new adventures.

He supervised a team of four other dog handlers, with the same regularization of typical days; in the morning feeding of the dogs at six o'clock, cleaning of the kennel at eight o'clock, followed by the training of the dogs according to the missions in progress.

For this four-month outdoor operation on behalf of the UN, one week of acclimatization in the theater of operation is enough for the dogs. Their diet is identical to their French habits:

croquettes and three bottles of water per day for the meal. They also add a daily tablet of Doxycycline to avoid malaria.

The dogs, very attached to their master, were ready to sacrifice their life, without any ulterior motive, in complete abnegation, because it is in their DNA to please the person who substituted himself the omega leader of the group.

They have inherited from their ancestors pack instincts based on hierarchical codes that remain strongly inscribed in them. The *"dominant"* behavior of the German Shepherd makes it an excellent fighting dog. Its bite, with a power of one hundred and sixty kilograms per square centimeter, equal to that of the Pitbull, can break an individual's arm bone. Its vivacity, power and absolute obedience to its master, propels it to the first place in the dog service of the army.

At the close of the *African Peace and Security* Summit in Paris, the President of the French Republic announced that 1,600 soldiers would be deployed for as long as necessary and that the mission of the French military was to disarm all militias and armed groups that were terrorizing the population. Finally, he confirmed that the French intervention would be rapid and effective, and would help restore stability and legitimize free and pluralist elections when the time comes.

At the end of the summit, *the African Union* decided to increase the MISCA force to six thousand men[16].

---

[16] Sangaris Operation by Wikipedia.

The instructions had been given and the briefing completed, and the dog handlers and their team members were free.

Joan enjoyed this special moment of calm and serenity that allowed him to be in perfect harmony with Syrius.

He isolated himself on a dune in the camp, facing the setting sun. He admired for a moment the regal attitude of his Shepherd, sitting upright, ears perked up, listening for the next command, eyes riveted on the horizon, ready to leap.

Syrius turned and stared at his master, as if a common thought was joining them.

The kindness in his dog's eyes made a blade come to the corner of his eyelid. He remembered this little ball of hair that had just been born and that he had been entrusted to make a soldier like him, he was then only held in one hand. How many paths we have travelled, how many missions we have carried out on all the battlefields around the world, and how many Islamists we have taken prisoner!

That made two brothers of love ready to fight.

General Abdallah Samba, a member of the Seleka, arrived at night, together with a dozen men, in the town of Bouca:

— Soldiers, we will show these Christian miscreants what we Muslims can do!

Immediately, he requisitioned motorcycles and asked the Muslim population for fuel and money to go fight the anti-balaka, who were mostly Christian.

Two jeeps, one of which was a pickup truck heavily armed with Kalashnikovs and razor-sharp cutters with which they cut open the bellies of pregnant women and took out the baby to

104

smash it on the mud walls of the huts. These barbarities had a precise meaning; *one does not attack the Seleka without suffering serious consequences.*

They left to attack the Bangui camp, located twenty-five kilometers from Gaga, in the province of Ombelle-M'Poko in the Central African Republic.

A few days later, Human Rights Watch, alerted by the local population, went to the devastated and burned mining village.

According to witnesses, the Seleka activists came and machine-gunned everything that moved. Several villagers tried to fight back but were unsuccessful, and Seleka members looted and then burned the houses.

Three corpses were reportedly counted by residents who remained in Camp Bangui, but Human Rights Watch assumes a higher death toll. The organization estimates that approximately 250 homes were destroyed and deplores the violation of international humanitarian law, as the participants in the attack were responsible for war crimes.

Joan Capdeverne heard the order issued; *"Gathering of officers and non-commissioned officers at the command post, immediately."*

The command center was in turmoil, as the HRW association had just made known the results of the attacks perpetrated by the Seleka militiamen.

Colonel Edouard W. of the BCAT reminded his dog-handlers of their instructions:

— Tomorrow at 6 zero zero, you will be in the area with your partners. You must protect your companions from a hostile crowd, remove and find the subversive elements.

For the rest, you know the orders, no shooting at civilians, just protect yourself! Do not forget the motto of the 132nd BCAT regiment: *"One against eight".*

Escorted by VAB armor, equipped with a turret gunner using an M2 (12.7 mm), the dog handlers are greeted by an angry crowd in Bangui. The predominantly Muslim residents pledged allegiance to the Seleka and raised their fists.

An armed pick-up with several fighters on board, placed in ambush, emerged from a hangar, machine-gunning at all costs. The VAB returned fire, the 12.7 bullets chopped it up and neutralized it.

<>

Joan Capdeverne rescued two wounded in the French ranks, including a dog handler, who were later repatriated to France.

A Kalashnikov bullet had hit the dog of another comrade-in-arms, Corporal Jean Delerme. He was devastated to see his faithful Shepherd dying. He raised his Famas Fl ready to fight. Joan jumped on him and turned the gun away; shooting at civilians was a Court-martial.

— Calm down soldier, don't risk the Military Tribunal. Get up and walk!

Jean Delerme lifted his bloodied companion in his arms, who was staring at him with glassy eyes.

He got into the VAB-VTT, for him the mission ended there.

— Well, soldiers, you know our mission; rid the population of rotten apples, find me the weapons caches, beware of children and women who hide explosives on them, you have been taught to spot them, and the sense of smell of our dogs will help you in this sense. We are here to secure the area!

A madman of Allah, his eyes hallucinated, came out of a hut with his arms in the air, brandishing a cleaver:

— Allahuakbar, allahuakbar (God is the greatest)

Joan made an instinctive shot, as she had practiced many times, Famas rifle on her hip, a series of six shots all on target. The jihadist bolted and lay there for the count.

All the inhabitants hid in their homes, the soldiers entered the houses, supported by a dog handler and his companion.

These Africans clearly did not notice that the French soldiers were there to help them and make them safe.

Ibrahim Ben Chouk was stationed on the roof, in an old reformed church, in the center of the city. His orders were clear, to do as much damage as possible to the ranks of the miscreant military.

In the distance, he saw the dust raised by the convoy of French tanks.

As a weapon he was given an RPG7 (rocket launcher), a Kalashnikov and an explosive belt in case he was caught. He knew that this was his last mission, so he might as well kill as many people as possible. And anyway, the ninety-nine virgins were waiting for him in Allah's paradise, he made a quick prayer and concluded "Inch Allah"[17].

---

[17] God is the supreme.

In his binoculars he saw the soldiers accompanied by the dog brigade. Suddenly, he caught sight of a dog that turned around and stared at him as if sensing the presence of an enemy and curled up its impressive lips.

As a result, Ibrahim broke out in a cold sweat on his back and flattened himself behind his low wall. He had always been panic-stricken by the wolfhounds of this regiment.

There were rumors that they were insensitive to mercy and that they would devour the heart of their enemy! He heard shooting at the entrance of the village, the fighting had started, he took the rocket launcher and adjusted his sight, the next few minutes were going to be decisive.

One of the jeeps turned off onto a sunny square, and stopped in a mineral silence. No noise, the dogs were at a stop, their ears pointed and their noses sniffing the odors of patchouli from a stall where the shopkeeper had disappeared.

The curtains were drawn on several stores, but there was no sign of a soul. Several samovars with tea still steaming were placed on tables, their occupants had left in a hurry.

Syrius pulled him back, sensing the imminence of a belligerent attack, and Joan immediately made a circle over his head, a sign of immediate retreat.

Looking up, he caught a glimpse of an orange flame from an overhanging roof. The impact on the front of the jeep lifted it and moved it twenty yards, turning it into a fireball.

Instantly Joan responds:

— It started from a roof located at ten o'clock, shoot it so we can dislodge the bastard!

A burst of several shots hit the roof from which the rocket had come, allowing Joan's team to enter the building.

Syrius and several dogs charged into the building, roaring, followed by their handlers and foot soldiers. No one was on the ground floor, but at each landing the dogs slowed down and went on the hunt again.

Syrius slowed down, he had sensed that the man on the terrace was full of explosives. Another dog overtook him, not listening to his master's orders, one floor below.

With a hellish growl, he jumped at the jihadist's throat just as he dropped a kalach' in his underbelly. They both died, their blood mixed, he will not go to the prophet's paradise being soiled by an animal.

Syrius did not emerge on the terrace, sensing that the matter was not over. Seeing his dog's hesitation, Joan called the bomb squad.

Those noticed:

— Luckily, your Shepherd sensed the problem, as the man was wearing a band of explosives triggered by movement and contact. If you had moved him, he would have jumped in your face.

The northern neighborhood was now secure, leaving the more Muslim and Islamized southern neighborhood.

At the corner of a street, the soldiers crouched down, they were crossing the southern zone, here people were going about their business, without any apprehension.

The jihadists melted into the population were much harder to spot. They could use civilians as human shields.

The soldiers in khaki and fatigues swore by their attire among all those djellabas. The women were completely veiled, only their eyes were visible.

Suddenly, there was silence. From a side street, a little girl of about ten years old moved toward them, her eyes unfocused. Her loose clothing could have hidden an explosive or a weapon.

The instructions were clear, a sniffer dog could be sent and lost in this case.

Victor Michaud, one of the masters, barked his order:

— Cassius, you go, my dog.

He shot off like an arrow, leapt on the girl and laid her in the dust. He smelled the feminine underwear, lifted with his nose the mini dress of bure, his examination finished he returned to place himself near Victor.

— The little girl is clean, sergeant, we can go on.

Joan thought that the jihadists were rather smart: sending a little girl and hoping that the soldiers would kill her, which would automatically start the hostilities.

He imagined his little girl Sandra being immolated for political or religious purposes, which would never happen in our democracy, what a barbaric people!

His attention was suddenly drawn to a glistening bead of blood on Cassius' muzzle, and Victor collapsing like a bloody rag doll. Instinctively Cassius the dog, lay on him protecting him with his body.

— Contact, Joan shouted, get down! A sniper is shooting at us.

He saw the corpses of Victor and Cassius, flinching from the impact of the bullets. They too will be buried next to each other.

— Who saw the start of the shooting.

— Me chief, says Ancelin Guillaume, at six o'clock, northwest. He did not put a cover on his telescope, the reflection makes a flash from time to time.

— OK, you protect us and we go. Go, go, go.

The sniper received a hail of bullets, forcing him to hide. Blocked in a minaret tower, he must have thought he was protected by the prophet, Ancelin took the LRAC FI rocket launcher and aimed it at him, triggering the shot.

Intended to destroy a tank, the rocket penetrated the rotunda of the tower, and decapitated it, raining down an amalgam of bricks and bloody flesh.

— Great shot, soldier Ancelin, the bearded ones will keep quiet now, Joan exclaimed.

A group of children emerged from a street, running with a soccer ball. They were passing the ball back and forth as they approached the soldiers. A teenager received the ball and threw it into the middle of the group of infantrymen.

The explosion took everyone by surprise, the children were still lying on the ground, stunned by the blast.

Thousands of impacts from screws and bolts speckled the walls and the body of a jeep.

Syrius groaned near his master, Joan lay in the dust, a large open wound on the side of his face, aware of the tragedy that had just unfolded and, stunned, tried to estimate his body damage. His head was buzzing, blood was clouding his left eye, he looked around at the men, all of whom were lying down from the blast.

He tried to stand up, without success, his lower body paralyzed by the impact on his skull.

Syrius' grunt put him on alert, the sluggishness of his legs worried him, he was easy prey for an enemy.

"His Famas had jumped away from his position, he was left with the Pamas automatic pistol stuck in his belt. Faced with a kalach", it was a lost cause; he might as well try to kill a donkey with a fig, as Ancelin the Corsican said.

A door creaked open on his right, two eyes gleamed in the darkness of the room, a bearded man in a djellaba looked at him and judged the opportunity to attack him because of his immobility. He came out like a devil from his box, brandishing a long curved dagger, ready to slit his throat.

Syrius leapt at the intruder, aiming at his throat as he had practiced. The bearded man plunged his knife into the dog's teeth before collapsing with his lower face torn off in a spray of blood.

Syrius crawled toward Joan, his hindquarters bloodied and paralyzed. In a last effort, he placed his front paws on his master protectively and his muzzle on his thigh. "There, my master, I have fulfilled my mission, I hope I haven't disappointed you too much" Syrius seemed to say, scrutinizing him with a kind look.

Joan could see the life going out of Syrius, and he patted him between the ears as he enjoyed it, *"My friend, you have been my best companion, and soon you will join the kingdom of the dogs, and perhaps we will meet there. Go to sleep now, I'm watching over you,"* he whispered.

Lying on the ground, Joan felt a VBCI armor roll in. He would be saved, but not his Syrius.

He had earned his return to France, unfortunately without his companion, who would be awarded the gold medal for courage and national defense, a distinction that was well deserved.

As for him, the army was over, he had had enough of defending his country, he had to retire.

But it was sure, his family would soon be enlarged with a four-legged friend, a German Shepherd puppy, that would be great !

Chapter IX
Willie, the Parrot of Gabon

Alex Callagan returned from the African military adventures and ended his story, moved by the courage and self-sacrifice of the dog soldiers, ready to die for their master. They had deserved their country.

After the noise and the fury of the weapons and the fights, the sweetness of life of the inhabitants of the PACA region *(Provence-Alpes-Cote d'Azur)* attracted him.

To me the olive groves, the pine forests and the lavender fields, he said to himself. The hotel La Bellaudière in Grasse was well named after the work of Bellaud de la Bellaudière. Between the sea and the mountains, in a green setting, a XIXth century house where Gérard Philippe, Auguste Renoir and many others stayed.

This would be his retreat.

Near the Perfumery Museum in Grasse in the Alpes-Maritimes, the city of flowers, there was a shisha and hookah bar. Warned by the neighbors of hidden work, the police were on the premises. Lieutenant John Carradine was counting the employees:

— Gentlemen, I count three waiters and two cooks, get me your IDs. And find me the boss!

— Chief, come and see in the kitchen, an animal in bad shape says a policewoman. I think it's a grey parrot from Gabon, I've often seen them in my native region, Gabon.

— Are you sure about this, Melissa?

— Yes chief, even that it is an endangered species protected by the Washington Convention.

The poor animal has its wings cut off and its body covered with fat, and it is plucking its feathers until they bleed, it is a shame to see that.

— Does anyone know what his name is?

"My name is Willie," said the parrot!

— Great, among all these immigrant workers, at least one knows his name," laughed John. "Come on, let's get these people on board."

At the Police Station, located near the Grasse Station, Melissa was degreasing Willie's wings and telling his story:

— He was walking on the kitchen floor because he can no longer fly. He quickly stated his identity and even told the colleagues *" What's the problem?"*

— We're not used to dealing with this, but he seized due to his poor general condition and the lack of any authorization to detain," said John.

An investigation has been opened for *"abuse by neglect"*.

In the meantime, we have notified the director Stéphanie of *"La Seconde Chance"*, the animal welfare center of the district of Grasse, route de La Paoute, so that he can be placed in an aviary with other parrots.

According to Stéphanie, Willie is a very intelligent bird, but he was dying in this shisha bar, where he had no water or food. In addition, the number on Willie's ring does not match the papers the owner provided to the police when he came to pick him up.

After some research, the real owners are found thanks to the ring. It is the Chenier family of Castellane in the Alpes-de-Haute-Provence, a distance of sixty kilometers separates the two cities.

<>

— Mélissa, what is the status of the Willie parrot investigation? asked Officer Carradine.

— Yes chief, the owner of the shisha bar Ibrahim Mamlouk was arrested, besides his worries with the concealed work, he wanted to recover the parrot. He had just bought it on *"le Bon Coin"* with its cage for the modest sum of six hundred euros, to the company "Animaux Exotiques".

This establishment based in Charleville-Mézières in the department of the Ardennes of the region of the Big East, does not exist.

A false invoice for the purchase of the animal was presented to us. We think that an illicit trade of exotic animals takes place on the Internet.

We will be more, with the real owners of the bird.

<>

Near the Camping of Lavandes on the road from Draguignan to Castellane, the path was marked by many balloons, it was the birthday of Karine Chenier. She was going to celebrate her thirteenth year and had invited many friends.

Her parents Karl and Édith wanted to make things big, to make her forget her misfortunes of the previous year.

116

During the 2018 Exhibition of Exotic Birds in Hayange in Moselle, Karine had been proud to present her gray Gabon parrot named Willie and his glowing tail feathers.

This exhibition had delighted the amateurs as well as the neophytes, the large arranged aviaries had attracted a good number of spectators.

The beauty, the shimmering colors, the intelligence of the birds had something to surprise.

A magnificent multicolored ara had obtained the first prize. From the *Psittacinae* family like the Gabonese grey parrot, this one unfortunately did not speak like Willie, who was very voluble.

Thanks to his diction; Willie had reached the third place on the podium and was proud to display his medal by singing the *Marseillaise* on Karine's shoulder.

Unfortunately, the three finalist parrots were stolen with their cages on the last day, during the wine reception prepared by the organizers in another room.

The police who were called to the scene spoke of a gang of exotic animal thieves. Passionate amateurs were ready to pay fortunes to possess a rare animal.

There was still a chance that the animal would not cross the border and stay in France where it would be resold on social networks, or through the internet.

For a year, Karine and her parents had been scouring the internet leaving desperate ads. Without success.

<>

Melissa, the police officer of the Grasse police station, succeeded in finding the owners of the parrot, thanks to the national veterinary file I-CAD, because a bird is as important to its owner as a cat or a dog.

They live much longer than our four-legged friends, almost sixty years, and bring joy and happiness to a family.

Stéphanie had told her that Willie's wing feathers should grow back within six months. The bird had exclaimed when she had checked the length of the feathers *"Oh the idiot... my wings"*.

Ibrahim Mamlouk didn't want Willie to fly away and had removed the feathers. Fortunately badly done, his tail would become again as beautiful as before!

Now there was one important thing left to do; to warn his owners.

Edith Chenier was in the middle of making arrangements for Karine's birthday when her phone rang.

"Ha, her husband had forgotten the shopping list again."

— Hello, yes it's me, who are you?

How can the police, the Grasse police station, not tell me that my husband has been messing around with the speed limit again?

WHAT, you found Willie, our Willie?

Listen, you're only an hour away from us, I'm coming! It's my daughter's birthday today and it's going to be the best present we can dream up.

<>

— Daddy, where did Mommy go? I heard her car start up and speed off. You know what's going on.

— Yes Karinette, she called me on the phone to tell me she'll be back in an hour, that you could start the celebrations without her.

— Ah, that's not true, always keeping us company in important moments.

But I don't care, I'm going to have fun with my friends, try to stay away Pà, adults are persona non grata.

Édith was on her way back home, light-hearted to have found her fetish bird.

"Willie will see Karinette again, Willie will see Karinette again," sang the bird to no end.

— Ah, do you remember your teacher's name?

"Mistress oh my mistress
Don't touch my braids[18]" Willie immediately starts to sing

— You're unbearable, little punk!

Punk, punk, punk

"It's so good when you play[19]" continues the bird.

Edith looked in the rearview mirror at the parrot doing Games in its cage, and leaning at every turn on its suspended swing, like in the movie *"The Birds of Alfred Hitchcock"*.

She had just left the eagle's nest village of Gourdon to join the Napoleon road that traces the D4085. On the slopes of the

---

[18] Mistress, song Emile and Images
[19] Punk, song Michel Berger

surrounding mountains, the bluish reflections of the lavender fields illuminate the landscape.

At Séranon, Edith turned left, towards the Caussols plateau, famous for its observatory.

She decided to stop in the parking lot, where a few cars were parked. She opened the door of Willie's cage, he was not in danger of flying away, to let him admire the view.

Tourists were admiring the funny singing parrot as they passed by the car. Édith picked up a large lemon candy and began to chew on it.

Willie jumped on her shoulder, making her jump and swallow hard. Stuck in her windpipe, the candy was choking Édith.

Willie, understanding the emergency, jumped out of the window into the parking lot. He saw the people around the car, spread his wing stumps, and shouted:
"Emergency, emergency."

A man, seeing that Édith was turning blue and had revolting eyes, took her out of the vehicle and performed the Heimlich maneuver on her.

He stood behind Édith. and wrapped his arms around her, squeezed her stemum and with his closed fist jerked upwards, ejecting the candy.

Recovering from her emotions, Édith thanked her savior, leaving him his coordinates so that she could see him again.

Explaining the situation of his daughter's stolen parrot.

— But madam, your parrot, it is it that saved you.

He jumped among our group, shouting *"Emergency, emergency"*.

— I believe that if he had known the gestures of first emergencies, he would be your saviour.

Your little companion is extraordinary, never let him go!

Chapter X
Jack, the Beagle-Harrier

Just goes to show, even a bird can be an excellent watchdog and a great rescuer. Parrots are very intelligent and feel the love of humans as a priesthood and are able, like any animal, to travel miles to see their master. On the other hand, they can tear their feathers off in case of disagreement, and dislike, until they die.

Alex unfolded his map of France, what would be his next destination? His index finger stopped at Belfort, in the region of Bourgogne-Franche-Comté. With its fifty thousand inhabitants, this beautiful town in eastern France was an excellent base.

The lion of the Alsatian Auguste Bartholdi, represented by a monumental sculpture in high relief, lying at the foot of the citadel of Belfort, seemed to look majestically at Geneviève Saint Arnold from its granite pedestal.

She sometimes came to remember the tragic events that took place there during the festivities, at the end of 2010, for the hundred and thirtieth birthday of the famous Belfort feline.

On December 31, the Saint Arnold family was counting down the seconds to the next year:

— Five, four, three, two, ONE... 2011... Happy New Year to all, shouted Thomas the husband!

Happy New Year! exclaimed the brothers Patrick and Henri! Throughout the weekend, animations were proposed, an evening show on Saturday evening in the Parc de l'Arsenal, followed by a Great Costume Parade on Sunday afternoon, composed of actors, artists, volunteers, elected officials and the inhabitants of Belfort.

All along the fireworks, concocted by the city hall and shot above the citadel and the lion, a big crowd moved on the Vauban ramparts, its fortified belt and in the old town.

The Saint Arnold family marveled at the dazzling glow of the rockets and light bombs that startled Geneviève every time.
— Be careful children, a pig would not find its young in this human tide exclaimed Thomas. It would not be a question of losing you.
Patrick is careful with your little brother Henri, we count on you.

The final of the fireworks was magnificent, the people flowed back towards the big city, jostling each other in a general euphoria.
Passing in the darkness of the citadel, Patrick was tossed in the bath of crowd and left Henri who laughed with the top of its five years, thinking of a game.
He ran towards a group of children and the night enveloped him.
— Henri, Patrick shouted, is coming back here.

The horns of a nearby carnival extinguished his screams. Only the parents arrived and joined Patrick to look for Henri, who had promptly disappeared.

It had been six months now that Geneviève had been going back once, a hundred times, a thousand times, hoping to see her child again!

<>

Louis Jolivet drove his powerful Mercedes 4x4 up the Avenue d'Altkirch and left the barracks of the thirty-fifth infantry regiment behind him.

As he left his office in the Faubourg de Montbéliard, a photo of his daughter was slipped under his windshield wipers with this terrible sentence on the back: *"Your daughter is in our hands, don't warn the police."*

He had accompanied her that morning to the Happy Park belfortain to celebrate her fifth birthday. Her school friends were there too, was it a bad joke? He was going to find out quickly.

It was the weekend and the entertainment park was full as an egg, dozens of children were running around, a few adults were trying to lay down the law, unnecessarily.

He entered a room decorated in the effigy of his daughter Betty, with multicolored balloons and tables set up with candy galore. He recognized his best friend.

"Josy, where is Betty? I don't see her," he asked.

— Hello sir, it's been a while since we last spoke.

Louis took a host aside and asked him the same question:

— No Mr. Jolivet, the children are free to come and go, she may have gone out, or to the toilet with an animator.

— WELL, listen, did everyone shout where my daughter Betty is?

All the hosts had gathered and Michel Canon, the head of the Park, had come to look for the girl.

— I don't understand what happened, we have a video surveillance circuit that we are reviewing right now with no results.

— Look, my daughter was dressed in a little pink dress, pink socks and pink ballet shoes. She should easily be visible among the other kids.

— A little girl in pink, I think I saw her going out with a group of moms says Michel, playing back the images:
"Here she is, holding the hand of a little boy wearing a baseball cap."

— "You mean we can go in and out of your amusement center like in a windmill," offended Louis!

— No, Michel said indignantly, at the entrance we print a mini stamp on the children's hands, so that they can enter and leave without difficulty.

But your little girl must have known the boy because she followed him.

In his pocket a text message squeaked on his smartphone:
"Remember, don't tell the police or anyone else."
Louis Jolivet suddenly remembered that he should not take the police or anyone else into his confidence.

— Listen Mr. Canon, there have been some misconducts in your amusement park, I reserve the right to notify my lawyers.

<>

In an old forest house, near Champagney, close to the village of Evette-Salbert, north-east of Belfort, a couple, Gaspard, Sylvie and their child Johnny, were having a conversation.

— I don't understand how you can be so stupid at ten years old Johnny, I warned you to go under the cameras and to be discreet.

— Well yes Pà, I had put on my baseball cap and nobody paid any attention to me, don't worry!

— Well, I worked on the construction sites in Jolivet, he's loaded with money, he'll give us some.

— Pà, you told us that we would get the money with little Henri, and it's been six months that we've been lugging him from one place to another, in the massive forest of Evette-Salbert.

— Listen Johnny, when little Henry was in your arms all teary-eyed, I saw the opportunity for us to make a big family. I always wanted many children, but unfortunately your mother can't have kids anymore. This kid I love him and he loves me too.

This kid doesn't cost us much, he eats like a sparrow and will make a playmate with little Betty.

Sylvie will take care of the girl, she found her a brood of kittens to keep her quiet. We hold the good end, now I am going to make a phone call to the father.

<>

Louis Jolivet had been living with his daughter Betty for five years. The mother had died in childbirth and left him this cute baby. He spent all his days between his work as a contractor and his beloved daughter.

He had taken a blow to the back of his head when he learned of this kidnapping. His kidnappers knew about his personal fortune and were trying to take advantage of it.

During a construction site, in a building to be demolished, his workers had found a bitch with a litter of puppies. Disturbed by the noise, she ran away with two puppies, forgetting one puppy. This one was sickly and without energy. Perhaps she thought that it would not live long, and that nature would take its course and leave it to die.

Warned, Louis took the puppy and cuddled him. He didn't like to see animals whimpering, should he hasten the end of his life by drowning him? The workers had filled a can of water to refresh him, this was the opportunity to prevent him from suffering.

Only the little dog came to life in his arms, and looked at Louis as his savior.

— What am I going to do with you, little pirate!

He took him to a veterinarian, who confirmed the good health of the dog, a poodle, in spite of a weak constitution, but which should quickly take again of the hair of the beast.

Betty was two years old and accepted with joy this small companion with four legs, merry and dynamic, she found him a name quite indicated Pirate.

Louis was thinking about this when his mobile phone rang:

— Hello, Mr. Jolivet, I hope you followed my instructions and kept quiet about our case!

— I don't know who you are, but you're going to get into serious trouble if you insist on keeping my Betty. Don't hurt her, or you'll be in trouble.

— Blah, blah, blah, keep it up and I'll send you a chopped off finger of your kid.

— NO, not that. I will obey your requests, but let me talk to him.

— I'm the one who sets the pace, so pack five hundred thousand euros in a travel bag. I'll call you back.

The three kidnappers were taking advantage of a moment of peace to make new plans.

— This kidnapping will be the high point of my career, says Gaspard. We're going to retire, no more messing around with crooks, no more pickpocketing and other fencing, we're going to go under the coconut trees, to enjoy the sun.

As soon as he drops his pezet', we leave.

<>

Lieutenant Paul Personne of the police station located a stone's throw from the Happy Park received a curious phone call from the park's chief Michel Canon:

— Hello, Lieutenant Canon, I am calling you following an incident that occurred two days ago in my center, during the birthday party of Betty Jolivet, a five-year-old child.

This little girl disappeared in the afternoon and of course we have been looking for her. Her father Louis Jolivet was present and seemed to be aware of this absence, because it was he who asked us where his child was.

On the surveillance video, we can see her leaving holding another child by the hand.

Instead of telling the police, he threatened us with the wrath of his lawyer. Isn't that weird?

I think he didn't tell us everything, did you receive a kidnapping request these days?

— Because you think it was a kidnapping? continued the policeman.

— Maybe I'm wrong, but I'd like to know for sure, as the reputation of my amusement park is at stake.

Paul Personne, remembered a case that had occurred during the festivities of the hundred and thirtieth anniversary of the lion of Belfort, six months earlier. A five-year-old child had also disappeared.

He looked at his faithful dog Jack, a beagle-hunter:

— What do you think about it, my friend?

I wouldn't be surprised if these two cases were simultaneous.

The beagle wagged his tail, all his senses on alert, had his master decided to leave his office and take him for a walk.

No, otherwise he would have unhooked his leash and his mastic-colored gabardine, Colombo style.

He rummaged through his papers and suddenly came up with a testimony that made him leave:

— Damn, but that's for sure![20]

He heard her open a drawer, the one of the sweets, *"great, I'm going to have a delicious meal"*.

Michel Canon was doing his accounting, when his phone squeaked:

— Hello, ah hello again lieutenant, what's going on? Yes, a child was holding little Betty by the hand, why?

Well, OK, I wait to hear from you.

Ah, he doesn't want to tell me anything, this Indian, he got angry and let's wait...

<>

Geneviève Saint Arnold was cooking dinner when a knock came at her door. She went to open the door and recognized the policeman with his Beagle, who had taken care of the disappearance of her child a few months earlier:

— Hello Lieutenant, what do you want?

— I would like to ask you a specific question; when Henry disappeared, you said that a child took him by the hand and took him away?

— Yes, Patrick's brother did see this scene. Do you have any other evidence to support my son's disappearance?

— Look, Madam Saint Arnold, it's too early to make speculations, but I need this clarification to solve an ongoing case.

<>

---

[20] Statement of the commissioner Bourrel of the television series *"The last five minutes"*.

Louis Jolivet was biting his nails thinking about his Betty in the hands of a crook who was talking about chopping off her fingers with an axe.

But which was the heartless individual who could express himself thus?

Pirate, his daughter's poodle, also seemed distraught. He was running around in circles like a soul in pain.

Suddenly, he heard a noise near the gate of his house. He went out quickly followed by Pirate who was growling.

A guy in a raincoat was standing next to his porch, waving at him:

— who are you, what do you want?

— Police, Mr. Jolivet, may I talk to you?

— What's going on, detective, was I driving too fast?

No, I'm with the criminal investigation department. Did your daughter Betty come back from Happy Park and could I see her.

Jolivet slurred and stammered:

— I don't understand what you are doing in my house, I am in good standing with the authorities, leave me in peace.

My daughter is with my family and will return in a week.

— Listen to me carefully. Michel Canon, the director of the amusement park, phoned me, explaining me the scene you made last week in his establishment by looking for your daughter Betty.

So, I repeat my question, where is your daughter?

At these words, Jolivet collapsed in the arms of the detective, crying his eyes out.

— They took away my Betty and ordered me not to say anything to anybody and especially not to the police. They even threatened to cut off her fingers with an axe!

I have to collect the sum of five hundred thousand euros and wait for their instructions.

I don't know what to do anymore!

— You should trust justice, Mr. Jolivet, I have solved several kidnappings and I intend to do the same with this one. The gang of small-time crooks will soon be locked up, believe me.

In order not to tip them off, we won't use the usual channels, sometimes they have a wiretap at the police station, so no trouble.

Me, I have the chance to go unnoticed with my dog Jack a beagle. I see that you have a poodle too and it's good that they are trying to get along.

Now, if you don't mind, I'd like to set up my base camp at your house, so I can get an overview of your captors' demands.

— Today I am going to give him the coup, and to claim the biffetons, no pity for Mr. Jolivet, says Gaspard.

— Do you think he was able to gather the money, asked Sylvie.

— He had better if he doesn't want to find his daughter in pieces!

Now, Sylvie, you go to the airport of Basel and get the plane tickets, like we said.

Johnny, you stay close to the kids. Be careful around them.

— Tell me, Gaspard, what do we do with the kids, then?

— What do you imagine Sylvie, we kill them, they know our faces, no witnesses.

— Well, you know what you have to do Louis, you take a big travel bag and you fill it with the tickets. We're going to embed a GPS tracker in the handles of the bag, so it'll be easy to follow it back to the kid.

Johnny had grown fond of children, he had seen his father cut the head off a chicken and skin a rabbit alive and told him it would be no harder to kill a kid.

When his father had the money, he would set the kids free.

— Mr. Jolivet, here is a small video of Betty holding the newspaper of the day. You have the money? Well, you are going to deposit it in a dustbin of the toilets on the A36 to the Autogrill Aire of the Door of Alsace South.

We know the place well, if there are police forces on the spot, your little one will be patient immediately.

We follow you with binoculars, be discrete.

— You heard that criminal, what should I do, Paul?

— You continue his instructions, your daughter is in good shape on the video, bring him the money in the famous bomb bag. I will track him down in my personal vehicle. Since he doesn't know me, I will come upon him by surprise. I will warn my men at the last moment.

<>

— Johnny, is your mother back? Ah, she's on her way back, she should be here in half an hour. I got the money son, a mountain of it. I'll come home and take care of the kids.

No dad, you're not going to hurt them. I like those two little guys!

— Listen boy, I can't leave any witnesses behind. You'll let me do it, they won't feel a thing.

Hanging up the phone, Johnny went to the kids.

— Hello Betty, Henri, we are going to play a game. Outside it's sunny, I'm going to take you to the forest, to pick fungus, it will be funny, you'll see.

<>

Gaspard arrived in a hurry at the forest relay. He hadn't liked Johnny's last words. He was able to ruin his perfect plan. Seeing him sitting on the threshold of the house, he breathed a sigh of relief.

Business continued. A second car arrived, it was Sylvie, returning with the plane tickets.

— Well, everyone is here, exclaimed Gaspard, go and get the children.

— They're not here, Johnny lamented, they're gone.

— You didn't do it son, we don't have time to look for them, pack up Sylvie and let's go!

<>

When he arrived at the rest area of the A36 freeway, Paul Personne immediately saw the catastrophe, a large empty bag was placed in the toilet waste garbage can.

The kidnapper had transferred the money to another container, so it was impossible to know where it might be.

When he came out of the toilet, he immediately noticed a tall guy carrying a large suitcase and getting back into a Renault Scenic. Luck continued to smile on him, he recorded the license plate number and warned his men to follow the vehicle.

Gaspard, Sylvie and Johnny had climbed into the Scenic and were looking for the last time at the forest house they were leaving. At the bend in the road, a multitude of police vehicles were waiting to apprehend them.

Masked men of the BAC *(Anti-Criminality Police)* surrounded the Renault and told them to get out with their hands up. Lieutenant Paul Personne took the floor:

— Where is the child Betty?

Louis Jolivet was at the four hundredths of a second, Paul the policeman had to warn him as soon as the place of the sequestration was known, and the minutes passed at a desperate speed.

— Hello, Louis, we have arrested the three people who held your child for ransom. Now, come with your poodle to the address I'm sending you by text.

Hurry up and I'll explain on the spot.

The police forces were combing the forest area, when Louis arrived. He was taken to the lieutenant who remained enigmatic:

— Betty is followed by a boy of the same age, Henri, who has also been sequestered for over six months.

Johnny, the son of the parents, had taken a liking to the children and did not want to hurt them, unlike Gaspard, the husband, who wanted to kill them.

For now, Johnny has freed them, and they are alone in the forest. With the help of your poodle and my beagle, we will find them quickly. Our canine brigade was contacted but they were at another site and won't be here for another three hours.

The three hours passed without any result on the exploration of the place. The night had fallen and the undergrowth resounded with the thundering Betty and Henri. The Beagle and the Poodle played in the leaves and the ferns but did not realize the services that they could make.

Many inhabitants had come to reinforce the town of Champagney, where could these children be?

Suddenly, the Poodle took off in the opposite direction of where Johnny had indicated and where the hunting was going on.

Louis followed Pirate, who seemed to know where he was going. Every once in a while he turned around, sniffed the air and then set off again. As they entered a clearing, a log cabin stood in the center. Pirate the poodle leapt into the doorless entrance, and disappeared into the darkness:

— Pirate my dog, you found me, I was afraid, so afraid! exclaimed in a small voice the little girl.

Daddy, my daddy, oh this is the best day of my life!

— Paul, the children are there unhurt further north, Johnny had sent us south. It was the faithful Poodle who found them, brave Pirate.

◇

On the front page, in the newspaper l'Est Républicain the next day, a headline read "A poodle finds a kidnapped girl and a boy kidnapped for six months."

Chapter XI
Aldo, the Malinois Shepherd

Two kidnappings solved by the poodle of his mistress, it is not however an extraordinary hunting dog, but the love of his family is essential for him.

Admirable stories are still to be discovered, where will my journey take me?

Alex Callagan remembered the beautiful years of the footballers of Saint-Etienne in the years eighties, the Greens as they were nicknamed, from the color of their jersey. Sant-Etiève or Saint-Tiève in Arpitan and Sainté in colloquial language, this capital of the Loire department, deserved a visit.

The Campanile Saint Etienne Est-Saint-Chamond hotel would be an excellent starting port.

One of the coaches of OSSE *"l'Olympique de Saint-Étienne,"* Claude Prigent shouted in his beard, what a team of broken arms on this detection footballers of the year 2018. Some heads emerged especially those born between 2009 and 2010.

His phone squeaked:

—Hello, Mr. Prigent, this is the police station on the Cours Fauriel, we have arrested your daughter Candice driving a Mercedes class C Cabriolet. Her young age of fifteen years does not authorize her to drive a car, especially not belonging to her. She was together with two adults of nineteen and twenty years old, and of course, no one has her driving license.

She specified that the car was a rental, were you aware of this?

— Not at all, she has already run away twice. I don't know what to do, she's in with the wrong people.

What is she at risk of? he asked.

— Because of her young age, she has extenuating circumstances, as this is her first arrest.

But driving without a license is a serious offense and not a traffic violation. Since the first of April 2017, a fixed fine of eight hundred euros is required.

If the owner of the Mercedes does not file a complaint, it will remain only a handrail.

In the Cotonne district, screams were heard in a Mercedes — Smart garage.

The owner Mark Wareberg asked:

— Where is my C-Class?

— Chief, replied Max, a grouch, "your son Noah took it to please his new girlfriend. They won't get far."

— I must remind you that it was intended for a *"delivery"*. If they get arrested, pray that the police don't search the vehicle. Heads will fall off!

A phone rang:

— Hello, yes it's me. How did you find my Mercedes? Where, the police station of the course Fauriel, yes I would find. While leaving, he hit the groupie badly, in the plexus *"not serious, huh!"*

◇

Claude Prigent was arguing with a policeman when Mark Wareberg entered the room.

He was an imposing man, a Caucasian from Tbilissi, whose real name was Kars Kalkas, short but wider than he was tall, with a mottled shirt over a hairy chest, jet-black curly hair with a very stylish back catogan, and a cavernous voice:

— I'm here to pick up my Mercedes and my son Noah. Where are they?

— Do you have your identity papers to show me please? said the policeman on duty, impressed. You can have your car back, but your son won't be out until tomorrow morning.

— Good for him, a night in jail can only put some lead in his head.

— What about my daughter, asked Prigent?

— Ah because it's your daughter who makes my Noah do stupid things, retorted Mark!

— Same, she'll be out tomorrow after seeing Lieutenant Greg Philipp, the cop said.

◇

The evening was well advanced in the Soulié street in the center-east of Saint-Etienne, when a fight broke out, undoubtedly on a background of drug debt. Last December, a dispute had already been settled with a hammer in a PMU bar.

The following Sunday, a violent brawl between two rival gangs, in the Cotonne district against the one in the Soleil district, ended in another kebab shop, under the fierce eyes of the manager, Khaleb, who was overwhelmed by the young people who started to fight outside, running back and forth, and then one of them came in, known to Khaleb, with a head injury.

He collapsed, in a pool of blood on the ground.

Then, other individuals entered the restaurant and started to break everything; they were bare-chested and they shouted while looking for the injured person. Khaleb Mamoud took out a baseball bat and cleaned up, from the top of his two meters and one hundred and thirty kilos, the giant fired everyone in petto.

His kebab was one of the places where drugs were supplied, the injured man was one of his dealers.

— Don't touch my stuff, he shouted to the neighborhood.

The residents of Louis-Soulié street became small, and went home.

Several complaints were made to the central police station, but none of them were resolved. *"Drug trafficking is done in broad daylight, exchanges between suppliers and consumers take place in the street and nobody does anything"* said a neighbor.

<>

A few meters away, near the church of Sainte-Barbe-du-Soleil, a man lay on the ground, hit by several bullets, he was dying.

— This dogfight must end, shouted Lieutenant Greg Philipp. It's another Adventist church takeover. Someone has an idea how to infiltrate the drug dealers.

— We could bring in the dog squad and their dope-sniffing dogs to find their caches, said Sonia Michaud, a new police woman.

— Well Sonia, let's put it all in order, we'll talk about it again tonight at the briefing.

<>

Mathieu Massue, dog handler of the canine team of the national police in Saint-Etienne, was training his Belgian Malinois Shepherd named Aldo, born in April, in his large personal garden, transformed into a training center.

His title of team leader and dog handler allowed him a few privileges, in particular to train his dogs in his private property. His malinois was sufficiently sharpened on the search/olfaction, the customs often made him intervene on explosive searches in the airports and especially the narcotics which he discovered at an amazing speed.

But now he was teaching her to overcome her apprehension at the sudden sounds of firearms.

After a one-week training course at the CNFUC *(national training center for dog units)*

The main mission of this unit is to support the other police officers, especially those of the police rescue.

They are sometimes confronted with risky situations that require the intervention of the canine unit.

142

"The dog has a dissuasive effect, it calms down aggressive people very quickly," Mathieu often said. The dogs are required for armed individuals, or those hostile to a police operation, or for people who are drunk, in a state of irritation, or during fights at the exit of night establishments.

If deterrence is not enough, the dogs of the squad can be used in a more offensive way; the attack is done with a muzzled dog or with a biting attack.

There the dog is fangs out, continues Mathieu. He had had the chance to finish weaning his four-legged companion and the latter looked at him with the eyes of Chimène, "Don't touch my master, otherwise beware!"

He had led Aldo on many missions, all successful.

The security service of the Saint-Etienne-Bouthéon airport had just called him to check the luggages of a private transit flight arriving from Marrakech. Terrorists and drug dealers often arrived from Maghreb countries. The new instructions from the Ministry of the Interior were clear, no special privileges, zero tolerance.

Air Arabia Maroc was stopped at the west end of the terminal, waiting for the border police to do their checks.

Several pairs, handler and dog, were already at work searching the luggages on the tarmac. Mathieu and Aldo's main role was to enter the plane and check the passengers. With his height of ninety-two meters and his weight of one hundred kilos, he was naturally imposing, walking in the central bay of the plane, all eyes were fixed on him, especially female. The women behind their veil appreciated this tall, dark-haired man with blue eyes.

Suddenly Aldo ran between the people seated and climbed on top of the seats, putting his ears down, which was a sign that he had found something. Mathieu opened the luggages container and took out several small suitcases. The dog jumped on one, sniffing;

— Whose suitcase is this, he asked?

— It's our turn, answered a couple of elderly people who were taken aback.

— Please follow me, sir, madam, he said.

He immediately imagined what he was going to find, drugs and these little old men serving as "mules" for a hashish smuggler, often without their knowledge.

Now the case did not belong to him anymore, it was the customs personnel who would take care of it.

He remembered Aldo's last discovery at Lyon-Saint Exupéry airport on a flight to Montreal Canada in North America.

Among the passengers, the dog had been interested in a British citizen named Richard Malwin, without luggage, which had surprised Mathieu for a flight to the Americas.

The screening machines didn't notice anything special, but Aldo couldn't stop smelling the suspect's shoes.

He was taken to an airport lounge and stripped naked. There, Mathieu found the terrorist's trick: an explosive in the sole of his shoe, *"penthrite"*, which could blow a hole in the plane's body and expose it in mid-air.

Richard Malwin was born of an English mother and a Jamaican father and lived in Bromley in Greater London.

He was a regular prisoner of various convictions and converted to Islam in 1995 on the advice of his father.

Upon his release in 1996, he attended the Brixton mosque, then the one in Fingsbury Park where the sulphurous extremist imam Abu al-Masri officiated.

This could only lead him to the path of Islamic extremists.

Searches at his home were conclusive, they found *"Al-Qaeda"* ads on his computer.

The American Airlines Boeing seven six seven carrying one hundred and ninety seven passengers that day owed a debt of gratitude to the French pair.

As was the custom, a guard of honor was formed in small groups. All the handlers of the service, followed by their binomial, greeted Mathieu and Aldo.

As a result of this incident, Aldo was nicknamed *"shoe bomber."*

In one of the cellars of the Kl building in the Couriot district, Djamel N'Dia was training his pitbull Lucifer on a rabbit skin tied and hung several meters high.

Soon a fight of dogs will take place in a secret place. Big stakes with lots of money. But above all, the honor of the gang was at stake, it was necessary to win!

Small and massive, the dog dashed forward and bit hungrily into the fur. When his mouth closed like pincers, he hung on and flapped his paws frantically in the air.

His buddies sometimes laughed at him when they saw him hanging from his pelt.

— Don't laugh guys, if she catches you, she'll stick like a mussel to her rock, it's like the cops

"ch'tharpogne and I don't let you go anymore" is her motto to Lucifer.

— Why did you name your giant dog Lucifer, it's a female?

— Barely born, she was already biting everything that came within reach of her muzzle, a real little devil. Enraged not a hair of tenderness! Her name was obvious, answered Djamel. She made me a litter of three puppies, I sold two out of the three, twelve hundred euros, it's a gold mine this animal.

She comes with me in my deals, with her collar with steel spikes and her patient head, the buyers are quiet and pay without discussion. It is cool !

<>

At the central police station Lieutenant Philipp was nagging his troops!

— Tomorrow at six o'clock, we invest the district of the street Louis-Soulié, the kebab restaurant and its manager maleb Mamoud, high place of the exchanges of dopes as well as his

apartment on the second floor will be our first target, the second will be the K1 building in the Couriot district, and the apartment of Djamel N'Dia.

We will be supported by the dog squad of chief Mathieu Massue. He brought us a lot of help lately.

We are going to give a kick in this anthill that is smashing our children, and leading them on the path to artificial paradises.

146

No need to remind you the orders, Khaled Mamoud is a giant of almost two meters, master him first then *"Visit"* thoroughly the apartment and the restaurant, we should find some surprises.

For Djamel N'Dia it is different, he is protected by his hound Lucifer, so beware.

◇

Khaled Mamoud was immersed in a wonderful dream, he was surrounded by sylphs and other nymphs who found him beautiful and who surrounded him with caresses and fiery kisses.

A girl of about ten years old, naked and drugged with GHB *(gamma-hydroxybutyrate)* shared his bed. He sometimes used this synthetic drug to achieve his goal, rape. The very interesting principle of this stimulant was that the victim had forgotten everything the day after the facts.

He did not see an endoscope *(wire camera)* sneaking under his front door and viewing the scene. At the other end, a policeman was watching on a monitor the movements in the apartment. Behind him, all the Raid policemen, in combat gear, were preparing for the assault. The canine squad was also ready to intervene.

A powerful stroke of a ram had broken down the door and about twenty masked agents quickly entered the place. Khaled's dream was abruptly interrupted by the police raid on his room.

He reacted instantly and swept the first men away like straws. About fifteen policemen finally immobilized him and put him in a straitjacket, dedicated to recalcitrant prisoners, following the orders of Lieutenant Philipp.

Mathieu Massue and his faithful Aldo found the numerous hiding places of cocaine, hashish.

— Rape, embezzlement of minors, suppliers of illicit products, attacks on persons in charge of the public authority; you are not close to see your restaurant again Mr. Maled Mamoud specified Greg Philipp.

The investment of Djamel N'Dia's apartment did not happen without breakage. The endoscope was torn off by the pitbull, the policeman had the time to see the inside of the mouth of Lucifer, before the rupture of the device.

The professionalism of the dog handler Mathieu Massue was put to the test. He knew how dangerous the dog was and he had prepared a lasso or pole, reserved for wild animals, because there was no question of shooting Lucifer if he could be re-trained.

Unfortunately it didn't work out so well for Djamel who was shot before he could use a Glock gun hidden under his mattress.

The drugs hiding places were also discovered, as well as a host lurking under the bed, a pitbull puppy that was entrusted to Mathieu.

For a long time he had been looking for a puppy of this breed to be his playmate.

Often assimilated *(wrongly)* to molossoids, the pitbull is a dog with a controversial character. It has a strong muscular body and a very lively air. It is an ideal dog for families with children, on the sole condition that it is adopted very early. With a good education that Mathieu will give him, his aggressiveness will be erased and it will present qualities of softness, calm and fidelity. A very good choice, even if each outing in public must be equipped with a muzzle and a leash.

Mathieu Massue had a second hat and also had the title of zootherapist, obtained by the French Institute of zootherapy in Lyon 2.

In addition to his qualities as a police dog handler, he also rehabilitated aggressive dogs that had been mistreated and channeled into dog fights by suburban thugs. Lucifer would soon be his next pupil.

Mathieu thought about this as he carried the puppy in his arms, he was going to join the group of his *"educated"* dogs on his property, the Labrador Retriever was the calmest, the big Saint Bernard was the clumsy one, a Saint-Hubert dog carried in his genes all the British placidity, an old and phlegmatic Great Dane completed the group.

When he incorporated a hyperactive dog into the team with the usual precautions, the troublemaker was immediately reassured and eventually calmed down.

In contrast to Djamel, who continually hit him to bring out his wild side, the puppy looked at Mathieu his new master, conquered by the kindness he saw in his eyes, his instinct told him that he could let himself go to the softness of these gestures.

— How shall I call you, little Chenapan? he asked. Yes, Chenapan, you seem to like it.

At these words, the puppy wagged his little tail and licked his hand.

Aldo sniffed the little pitbull, gave a big lick to welcome the newcomer, already protective towards a smaller one than himself.

Chapter XII
Coquin, the Labrador

Some dogs are not only apples of love and tenderness, they are also animals that can become wild in the wrong hands and under the wrong owners. Don't we say that who looks like, comes together, and that we recognize the owner to his dog.

Chenapan, the little pitbull, will surely become an adorable pet dog.

Alex Callagan came out quite upset by the drama of this story.

His index finger lingered for a moment on the region of Bourgogne- Franche-Comté, in this beautiful town of Villeneuve-sur- Yonne. A hotel answering to the sweet name of the "trois roses" would be his temporary halt.

It was the holydays, a hot summer was coming and Francis, Mariette and the youngest Johnatan Leboeuf were planning to enjoy the nice days at the campsite Le Saucil in Villeneuve-sur-Yonne.

Johnatan was eight years old and was followed by his faithful labrador Coquin, who followed him like a shadow wherever he went.

Francis, the father, had booked six months in advance, a more comfortable mobile home than their last tent, which had flown away the previous year, taking all their possessions with it.

Located five hundred meters from the city center, close to all the shops, a market twice a week for shopping, a supervised lake for swimming, this campsite was ideal for the Lebœuf family's small budget.

Mariette, who was a fan of old stones, would visit the medieval city as well as the Notre-Dame church *(13/16ᵉ century)*, the surrounding towers, the Saint-Nicolas bridge. Enough to feed her historical deficiencies.

For eight years Johnatan and Coquin had been living a tender story, where complicity was mixed with love. The labrador had been offered to them as a baby, from a litter of six puppies, he was the quietest and the most affectionate, perfect for their newborn Johnatan.

Better than a cuddly toy, Coquin was the one who could heal the child's soul. It was to him, this doggie with all ears, wet nose and wet eyes, that he confided his sorrows.

Francis was always surprised to see him pull his hair and tail. Brave, the animal did not flinch; neither plaintive barking nor threatening growling.

Faithful companion of play, untiring, Coquin was protective and reassured Jonhatan, Francis and Mariette often said that it was their second child.

◇

The Rescue Center on the Saint-Nicolas suburb was busy preparing for the hot and sunny days that are fateful for some elderly people and also for children.

The previous year, numerous cases of sunstroke and forest fires had put the firemen to work.

No one was hurt, so the chief of the center, Stéphane Benas, the only professional among the forty-five volunteers, wanted to repeat the same results this year.

More than a thousand interventions over the two semesters, it is true that they were not unemployed, the firemen.

Since a few months, the fire station had welcomed a mascot in the presence of a small dog.

The municipal policemen had asked the chief Stéphane if he wanted to adopt a female labrador.

Once said, once done. The animal was accepted by the team, with the sweet name of *"Perle."*

Helpful in difficult neighborhoods, she calmed overexcited people and took care of unruly children.

Martine Louvel's veterinary clinic was always full. From Piggy the Pig to Pouf the horse, each owner knew Martine the vet as the savior of the sick animals.

They came from all over the department and sometimes further away, to follow the young woman's enlightened advice.

The fire department had called her to establish a partnership to finance part of the care and feeding of the canine.

Stéphane Berras had already used Martine Louvel's services, but as a private owner.
Especially since he had just lost his poodle to a vehicle that had not stopped.
The veterinarian knew Stéphane's love of animals and gladly accepted the association with the firemen of his city.

<><>

The Ker-Yonnec clinic on Route 70 treated addicts and drug addicts, many of whom came to this psychiatric clinic on their own.

A former volunteer firefighter, Miguel Sanchez was a pyromaniac and had an impulse characterized by an extreme fascination for fire, this monomania was translated into impulses pushing him to cause fires as an outlet for excess tension that triggered relief and gratification *{Ex. Wikipedia}*

Stéphane Berras, his boss at that time, had noticed the worrying glint in Miguel's eyes during the forest fires around Villeneuve-sur-Yonne.
He finally thanked him and sent him home, asking him to get better.

Returning to his little house on "rue de la Châtelaine" in Rousson, he went to see his two cats and Oscar, his French bulldog, his only true friends in life

"Why are people so wicked to me, can you answer me Oscar?"

Sanchez had been locked up during the day and on his own.

He had found his vocation, to be a firefighter.

He had to regain the confidence of his chief, Stéphane. He had never been caught in the act, during the fire starts.

There was a lot of talk about the psychiatric services at Ker-Yonnec. It will take as long as it takes, he thinks.

Stéphane Benas, at the beginning of August, had decided to take his day off at the Saucil campsite. Obviously he was on call, in case of a big blow, he would be mobilized quickly.

The head of the camp was a friend, so he kept a tent for him all year round near the mobile homes.

He could swim with Perle, his Labrador retriever, in the big pond without bothering anyone.

He came out of his tent when he heard barking, he thought he had a vision when he saw two labradors having a party. A young boy was trying to separate them without success.

— Coquin, stop playing the fool, come here!

— Perle, that's enough, heel! he said, laughing as the dogs were having fun together and not fighting.

"So, young man, this is your dog too?"

— Yes, sir, I think they're getting along and getting to know each other. My name is Johnatan and this is Coquin.

154

— Well, you are in presence of Perle, my female Labrador.

<>

Miguel Sanchez had just spent a semester in the specialized clinic and his demons seemed to have vanished. The head of the department, Liliane Pages, had warned him that he should not feel he was out of the woods, that his impulses could return and that it was a long process.

Nevertheless, he was able to return to his former profession.

The same day, a fire broke out in Rousson on the D15, a quarter of an hour from Villeneuve, and ravaged twenty-five hectares of fields. A few houses were affected on rue de la Chatelaine, but one was completely destroyed. About sixty inhabitants were momentarily evacuated by the firemen and the police, their houses being close to the fire.

The investigation carried out by Stéphane Benas and the chief brigadier of the gendarmes did not have much difficulty in determining the origin of the fire.

Marks of hydrocarbon had been found in several points. A cigarette butt thrown carelessly through the door of a car, on the dry grass like oakum, ignited the field.

Miguel was arrested immediately, and Stéphane made him climb into the van of the barracks:

— We just put out the fire, Miguel. You are still impregnated with this gasoline, you are a sick man. It was brought under control after ruining a house in Chatelaine Street, you know which house I mean, *"Yes"* yours.

The corpses of the animals buried between four walls, the scratches on the doors show the slow agony they have endured.

— NO, my cat friends, my beloved bulldog, my God what have I done?

With these words, he jumped out of the fire truck, took out a lighter and lit himself on fire with the gasoline he had on his clothes. The fire ran down his body and engulfed it in flames.

The fire was doused with dry ice and smothered, but not fast enough to save Miguel, who died on the spot from a heart attack.

— It's better for him, third degree burns on more than ninety percent of his body are fatal, Stéphane said.

I just found in his car, the agreement of Liliane Pages, the head of the Ker-Yonnec clinic, to resume his job as a firefighter.

She will hear me, that one!

<>

On the beach of Saucil the two labradors got along like pigs.

Not far away, Francis and Mariette, Johnatan's parents, were sitting with Stéphane, having an aperitif under the high wind of their mobile home, which was next to his tent.

Johnatan was watching the two dogs, having fun throwing a stick and seeing who would bring it back first.

The heat of the late afternoon was still stifling so he got into the water too.

A rabbit ran away from the dogs, who immediately chased it into the bushes, leaving Johnatan behind.

Diving from a pontoon bridge, Johnatan entered the icy water and felt a shock of electricity. The hydrocution surprised him and paralyzed him. The thermal shock immobilized him between two waters.

Stéphane was the first to notice that the barking of the dogs seemed far away.

— Why do I hear the dogs in another part of the beach? he exclaimed.

He stood up quickly followed by the parents who were getting worried.

— Johnatan, JOHNATAN, shouted Francis the father.

The dogs had returned, circling, looking for their little master. Suddenly Coquin ran along the beach and dived off a pier.

Stéphane followed him and dived in turn, bringing back Johnatan in a purple color.

Immediately, he gave him mouth-to-mouth resuscitation and pressed on his chest, compressing his sternum in a regular rhythm:

— Johnatan, come back to us, come back...

He continued for thirty minutes, accompanied by the rescue team who took over.

He knew that it was too late, he had already rescued drowned people and he knew the symptoms of fatal hydrocution. A few minutes of inattention were enough to drown a child, and especially in silence, without any noise.

The next day, a headline crossed the front page of the Yonne Républicaine *"A child drowns at the Villeneuve-sur-Yonne bathing beach on the Saucil beach."*

Two days later, Francis called Stéphane:

— Hi Stéph, something incredible happened last night. I heard Coquin the labrador scratching at the door of the mobile home. I opened it for him and followed him to see where he wanted to go. He ran along the beach and I saw him dive off the dock where my son had drowned. At one point on the sand, I called out to him, he turned around, looked at me and continued. I saw him swimming and all of a sudden he sank, just like that...

What do you think?

— Listen Francis, your son and Coquin were very close. He probably couldn't bear the loss of his little master and wanted to join him. This is a great act of love.

— Yes, but we have nothing left to love...

Francis and Mariette had shut themselves away in their living room and were watching the latest Johnatan and Coquin film running through the autumn leaves in their garden with tears in their eyes.

The service of the priest of their parish had not been able to comfort them enough. How to accept the departure of Johnatan, followed by Coquin? It was as if they had lost both their children.

The phone rang in the entryway, making them shudder:

— Hello, Francis, it's me Stéphane, please put me on speaker. I have good news for both of you; Coquin knew what he was doing when he left to join your son, he wasn't leaving you alone.

My Perle is going to make little Coquins, I suppose I'll keep one or two of them for you?

158

Chapter XIII
Tyson, the Sharpei

The love of Coquin for Johnatan was a divine act, some people might think, the sublimation of the impulse of Coquin to join Johnatan in the abyss is fundamental and incomparable.

Alex left the hotel of the three Roses a little distraught, snorted and left his emotions behind him.

A next step was taking shape on the map of France spread out before his eyes. Nancy, the city of the Grand Est, in the northeast of France, is known for its late Baroque and new art style sites. The Ibis hotel at the Center of the Station and Congress seemed ready to welcome him.

The roar of the motorcycle fills the air.

The neighbors of the car pound on Boulevard Jean Moulin on the edges of the Moselle in Nancy were used to it and recognized the exhaust of the Harley-Davidson and the softer Suzuki of the married Xavier and Cendrine Poljack.

They were returning to their house located at the bottom of a garden full of wild grass. They brought their bikes in under the lean-to that served as a garage for their Harley and Suzuki.

Xavier was alone on his bike, but Cendrine was carrying young Kevin behind her Suzuki.

A little dog, all wrinkled, came out of the grass and came to celebrate a party :

— Tyson, where did you come from, you're all steamed up, you went to the neighbors' to see your girlfriend Erika again, scolded Cendrine!

— Leave him alone, said Xavier, our sharpei is living his dog's life. I would like to have the same one, too.

Kevin took his dog in his arms, full of attention, caressed him and hazed him.

Other motorcycles stopped in front of their gate, in a hell of a noise.

— Hi guys, you are early for the barbecue!

— Oh Pà, you thought of celebrating my birthday with your biker friends, that's great! he said from the top of his ten years.

<>

A husband and wife entered the emergency room of the Central Hospital on Avenue du Maréchal de Lattre, the man carrying an unconscious child in his arms.

— Quickly, my boy passed out for no reason, I came as quickly as I could.

— Sir, a nurse said, you should have called the ambulance or the fire department, which have the necessary equipment for first

160

aid. He could have had a cardiac arrest in your car and you would have been in big trouble.

Nevertheless, we will take care of him immediately. Lay him down on the stretcher. Then go to admissions and check in.

— Mr. and Mrs. Joubla, I am the doctor Simon the emergency doctor on duty, your child Ahmed suffers from cervical disorders, he is awake and complains of headaches. Has this happened before?

No, said Karim and Larissa together. Our son is about to turn ten, and we were all sitting at the table when he was starting to vomit and he felt bad. We came straight here. We live near the Place Stanislas in the center of town.

— Here is his health booklet, said Larissa the mother. Please give us good news, Dr. Simon.

— Mr. and Mrs. Joubla, we performed a scanning procedure which revealed a disturbing mass near the temporal lobe that will require further investigations.

The Poljack family received a letter from the prefecture of Meurthe-et-Moselle, an operation *"Responsible Motorcyclists"* was organized this Saturday to sensitize the amateurs of two wheels to the codes of good behaviors and to the prevention of the risks when one rolls to motor bike.

The event took place on the Zenith parking lot in the northwest of Nancy, near the Haye forest.

— I have registered you Cendrine, says Xavier, with your Suzuki Bandit 600, review some rules will not hurt you!

(Laugh)

She replied:

— Why don't you go too?

— With my super trapp mufflers, too noisy, I have no chance to be retained in the training workshops of the road safety.

Besides, I am a biker, a rebel, I prefer to avoid the police. Besides, at the Harley club I don't want to be laughed at, I don't want to be seen to be fooling around with the police.

You, you're a princess of the road, you won't be blamed for anything, baby!

I would take the opportunity to take my Kevin for a ride.

— Hello, this is Samu Center 15, how can I help you?

— My name is Henri and I have just witnessed an accident on the national road 57 near Champigneulles. A motorcycle missed a turn and crashed into a field, the driver and his young passenger were ejected, hurry up!

The firemen arrived on the spot and took care of Xavier and Kevin.

Xavier had rolled over and got off scot-free with a few scratches, only Kevin deserved more attention from the doctors. Both were taken to the emergency room of the Central Hospital.

— I'm sorry, son, that I made you take a partnership ticket, but I wanted to avoid a rabbit that was running out in front of us and sent us into the cornfield.

I'm going to be scolded by your mother, that's for sure!

— It's not your fault, Pà, don't worry, I'm already better.

Xavier had come out of the medical examinations without any problems and was waiting in the waiting room of the hospital, when he heard the muffled sound of the Suzuki's mufflers.

— Xavier, what did you do to my son? she raged.

— It is also mine, he retorted, the doctors are flattening his arm, he fell badly and cracked his radius. He has four weeks of immobilization.

He is already thinking about the many dedications that his friends will draw on his arm. YOUR son is very brave!

◇

Karim and Larissa were devastated. The head of the oncology department, Julien Labranche, had just given them the terrible diagnosis that their child Ahmed had cancer of the left temporal lobe.

It was going to be necessary to do surgery on him, and to make him undergo a whole series of painful and unpleasant tests.

"Above all, don't hide anything from him, tell him the truth, continued the professor, children can sense when they are being lied to!"

They joined him in his room:

— Mom, dad, a nurse looked at me with a pitiful look, what's going on?

— My child, the doctors have diagnosed a nasty disease in your head, you will have to be strong and we will fight this tumor with you my son.

◇

In a hospital room, Kevin was staring at his arm in a cast, already autographed by every nurse on the floor.

— Ah, you can say that you made us a beautiful fright my beloved, sobbed Cendrine.

— Don't cry Mum, I'm doing fine, and it's not Pà's fault that we had a nice tumble. A stupid rabbit tried to overtake us and Pà avoided him and we found ourselves ploughing the field with the Harley!

— Yes son, you have summarized our epic well. Give me your arm so I can draw you a big heart, next to your mother's.

After leaving Kevin in good hands at Central Hospital, Cendrine and Xavier returned home. Their neighbor Sarah was waiting for them:

— So it's not too bad, the flying of the pitchoune.

What an adventure!

Well after this good news, I have another one that will make you happy. Tyson is having an affair with my little Erika, she is going to have puppies. As they are both shar-pei, we will have cute Tyson.

Little balls of fur all crumpled up.

Hallelujah!

— Dad, Mom, I dreamed of Uncle Mehdi and his big motorcycle, who would come to see me and take me for a ride.

— No Ahmed, my brother is abroad, I can't reach him, I know he loves you very much. He will reappear when we are not expecting him!

Julien, the oncologist, warned Ahmed's parents that he would be combining chemotherapy and radiotherapy to shrink the tumor and that he might lose his hair.

This would only be temporary and children, especially boys, were not concerned about their physical appearance during their illness. He could wear a bandana that would make him look like a pirate during this time.

<>

Mehdi had just finished his Moroccan trekking, in the foothills of the Anti-Atlas, from Douar to the Berber village of Tizgui, a true haven of peace in the middle of the palm grove. Full of memories, he returned to Agadir, the capital of the province of Ida-Outanane.

He had settled in the hotel Kenzi Europa located near the green corridor of the Valley of the Birds on the boulevard of August 20. After a good shower, he consulted his emails punctuated with professional alerts.

He immediately noticed his brother Karim's e-mail address and the blades came to him as he read the brief missive

"Come back soon brother, our little Ahmed is condemned by a bad disease and he is asking for you".

<>

Kevin's parents had negotiated with the hospital staff to bring Tyson the shar-pei to make him happy. He had been asking for his dog for several days and the surprise would only be better.

— Tyson, come here my dog, oh, Mà, Pà I missed him too much.

165

— Yes, since you've been here, your dog is unbearable, always in our paws, looking at us with sad eyes, whining and growling.

Two days ago, he did his business all over the house, when he usually goes out by himself. It's about time we took him away, I think he would have ended up biting us, laughed Xavier.

Suddenly Tyson jumped off Kevin's bed and ran to the open bedroom door, stopping on the threshold with his tail wagging. In the hallway, Ahmed was standing holding his drip in one hand and with the other caressing Tyson who had come to meet him. Completely bald, he was wearing a superb
multicolored bandana:

— Oh how cute you are, where do you come from sweet little dog?

— His name is Tyson. And you, who are you? says Kevin, I've never seen you on this floor?

— My name is Ahmed, I am a cancer patient undergoing chemotherapy. I need a companion like that because my days are long without friends to talk to.

— Well listen, I get a little lonely from time to time too. Come to see me when you want.

Back in his room, Ahmed reported the meeting he had made at the corner of a hallway:

—Mom, Dad, I would so love a little dog like Kevin's on the second floor.

And her parents are so nice, they didn't look at me and talk to me like I was sick. I'm sure you would like them too.

— Yes, we met them with your mom, Karim answered, and they made a nice impression on us.

166

As for their little dog, it's a Shar-pei. We will look for one for you, when you will have the permission to go out. As it is a very valuable dog, we will have to be very careful about the acquisition.

— Oh, it's already much better. Doctor Julien confirmed that I will be able to go out at the end of the week, for the weekend.

◇

The sun was shining on the airport of Metz-Nancy-Lorraine at the beginning of the weekend. The Agadir-Metz flight had just landed, a colorful crowd was pouring into the arrival hallways.

Mehdi had just spoken to Karim on the phone, his nephew had returned home, he was going to surprise him.

◇

Ahmed and his parents were taking advantage of his leave from the hospital and had just scoured the SPA, the Verlaine en Haye shelter, the Chat Botté and the Pension alimentaire du Grand Nancy in search of a shar-pei.

The few animals found did not seem to please Ahmed. He couldn't find the spark he had felt with Tyson.

He was desperate to find a companion who could make him forget his illness, and decided to return to the hospital.

◇

Xavier had found and repaired his Harley, which had lain in the grass after he had thrown them off.

Ah, my pretty one, I was afraid to have lost you forever.

After my son and my wife, you are my queen.

Come on, let me ride you and let's go get my Kevin.

Xavier and Cendrine arrived together at the hospital preceded by a cab.

Kevin and Tyson were waiting quietly in the big waiting room of the reception.

Ahmed, the drip-friend, had large bistros under his eyes and was also waiting, sitting next to his parents.

— I will miss you my friend, and so will Tyson your four legged friend. I tried to find the same dog, and I couldn't.

I believe that there is only one Tyson in the world and that makes me despair, he lamented.

— Listen, Ahmed, I'll come back every week to check on my cast, I'll come to see you and Tyson, I promise.

Xavier went to take care of the last formalities and came to discuss with Ahmed's parents:

—Hi Karim, Larissa, according to what you told me, it is Ahmed's birthday in a few days, why don't you come and celebrate it at home, our two children love each other very much and I would like to keep this beautiful growing friendship.

I asked Ahmed's doctor, Professor Julien Labranche, for permission and he has no objection if his health allows it.

He said that being surrounded by people who love him can be the best therapy.

A pale autumn sun was rising over Nancy, except in the Poljack home, they had warned the neighborhood that the weekend would be noisy with music, motorcycles, laughters and probably tears. A sick boy was coming to celebrate his tenth birthday.

A cab arrived and dumped Karim, and Ahmed without his drip, permission for the evening.

A dozen motorcycles cluttered the boulevard in front of the house which shone with the thousand lights of the lanterns placed here and there by Cendrine and Larissa. The two women had quickly become friends and had prepared things in a big way.

Karim let Ahmed be filled with the joy of finding his friend Kevin and Tyson who jumped like a goat to see him.

Rock music filtered from the living room where couples were dancing, a huge banner hung on the front of the house
"Welcome and happy birthday, Ahmed."

He went forward a little intimidated by all these people who looked at him kindly with amenity.

In a corner, a lot of presents were waiting to be opened.

In the center of the room, a large table covered with delicious food was set up with a huge cake in the middle.

— Well gentlemen, ladies, the king of the evening is in front of you, I present you Ahmed exclaimed Xavier.

One of his dreams is to ride a motorcycle, who is going to do it?

That evening, Ahmed rode as many motorcycles as he wanted.

Among the gifts he discovered as he went along, a shoebox with a red ribbon around it intrigued him. What could it contain?

When he opened it, a shar-pei took out his little face, had a smile on his lips and jumped in his arms.

— My God, a puppy like I dreamed of, but where did he come from?

— You have the pleasure of having the first of Tyson and Erika's litter, his shar-pei parents said Kevin.

— Thank you my friend, it's more than I expected!

Outside, a motorcycle humming came to cover the conversations, two gas blasts like his uncle Mehdi used to do in the past.

— Where is my favorite nephew, thundered a stentorian voice?

Chapter XIV
Magnus, the Doberman

The love of an animal transcends the illness of its master, makes him forget the pain and thus hopes for a future recovery. Isn't this the best remedy that every cacochyme wishes for his immediate future!

Alex moved away from the city of the duchy of Lorraine, towards a new stage.

Michel Delpech sang enough that his family lives in the Loir-et-Cher, Blois is a town located in this department and deserved a small detour, a stop at the Ibis Blois Centre Chateau to put down the bags.

Gérard, born in the fifties, remembered an almost unpleasant episode in his life as a young man, when he rediscovered the Maurice-de-Saxe barracks, near Avenue Maunoury and Boulevard Vauban, close to the royal castle of Blois.

Named CS 10 *(selection center)* and the place where the famous *"Three Days"* of soldiers doing their national service, which began in 1905 and was suspended by President Jacques

Chirac in 1997, were performed by Gérard in his twenties, along with hundreds of other young men.

Received by a guy who had to earn a few stripes *(oh, very few, he was a sergeant something)* with a big mouth, bellowed in the ears of the conscripts to sit in silence and he screened a short film about the benefits of the military on their future.

Vast subliminal and interminable smoke that Gerard had to ingest and regurgitate during seventy-two hours this compulsory military time.

Nostalgia deserved to be dwelled on.

It was dark on the square of the Royal Castle.

The House of Magic Robert-Houdin stood on its two floors, one window was brightly lit.

Roger Hitmann, the administrator of the Museum of Prestidigitation and Illusion, was working on the final details of the theatrical performance scheduled for the next day. The three hundred and fifty seats of the hall were rented for a comedy show *"Ten Years of Marriage"* with Alil Vardar.

Magnus, his Dobermann, was watching over his master, lying down on the inlaid parquet floor, his ears pointed at him, attentive to his every need.

He waited patiently for Roger to turn off his computer and the lights in the room so he could take his daily walk in the Valin de la Vaissière square.

The nearby park was their usual place, he could chase squirrels and wild cats without being admonished by the neighborhood.

Muscular body, high on legs, black as soot, a mouth full of fangs, people would move aside when Magnus passed.
Roger took advantage of this to keep order in the museum.

The premises of the Blésoise Gendarmerie on rue Signeulx resounded with cheers of honor launched by the personnel to the new captain Luc Boullot taking up his duties.

A first ceremony had taken place at the Chateau de Chambord, traditions oblige, the new commander was promoted in this prestigious setting.

With his sword in the air, the officer presented himself in a ceremonial uniform in front of a platoon of gendarmes from his unit and symbolically took command by having them present their weapons, then stand at the attention.

The horse unit of the gendarmes was also dressed up nicely and the horses were pawing impatiently and kicking the ground with their hooves.

A smell of horse manure was catching in the throat as soon as you entered France-Haras on Avenue Maunoury, where the horses of the gendarmerie were bred and trained.

Grégory Hitmann, one of the lads *(stable boys)* in charge of the well-being of the occupants of the stalls, looked after, broke in, and took a liking to these magnificent animals.

He took great care of Apache, a gelding with a black coat, good balance, muscular and racy.
"He is an extraordinary horse, intelligent, who knows his beauty and plays with it," explained Gregory.
He often dreamed that he was riding Apache into the sunset, like a certain cowboy on his Jolly Jumper.
Gregory was weak, short and sixteen years old. Most of the lads were teenagers, young people who took better care of the horses than the adults, a fact that every stud owner knows well.

Apache, the beautiful gelding had taken a liking to Gregory and quivered every time he brushed him, and couldn't stand to have another lad touch him.

On the castle square, the evening had fallen and the dragon animated the front of the illusion museum with its six heads.
Dating from 1856, this large building is the only public establishment in Europe presenting in one place magic collections and a different show every year.

Roger Hitmann was proud to be its representative. From Harry Houdini, the American magician nicknamed *"the king of escapism"* to Garcimore the Frenchman, spaces were dedicated to them and amazed thousands of spectators.

Sound effects and monumental video projections transform the walls of the museum. Roger was always amazed by the show telling the mysteries that have shaped the history of France, striking realism thanks to new technologies.de video mapping; a collapsing castle, a trembling Catherine de Medici or a Duke of Guise more alive than ever[21]

Roger thought about the beauties of life in Blois, and how lucky he was to see them.

Magnus the Dobermann had gone into the dense bushes on the trail of a playful rabbit, and had gotten away from Roger. The Garenne had returned to his burrow and was safely camouflaged, while the dog sniffed in frustration at the entrance to his den.

Further on, under the undergrowth, a drama was unfolding. Three armed individuals were demanding his wallet from Roger.

While one of them robbed him, the two others attacked him, leaving him in a pool of blood.

Magnus, seeing that the game was not moving, finally got tired and left to find his master. He came upon a clearing where Roger lay lifeless.

Sensing that something bad had happened, he screamed for death as he stood guard beside him.

The police forces of the Quais Saint-Jean police station, warned by the neighborhood, had surrounded the square Valin de la Vaissière with a security cordon.

The last aggression was several months old and had been carried out under the same conditions. This made Joakim Sanders, the police captain, wonder.

The director of the house of magic was on life support after the multiple blows he had received.

Strangely enough, his Dobemann had not protected him from the thugs, while he had been impossible to approach by the police.

Joakim had been forced to anesthetize him with a hypodermic needle.

Locked in a cage, Magnus spun around and grunted at anyone who approached him.

Suddenly, he fell silent and looked sharply at the police station door.

This one opened wide on Gregory Hitmann.

Roger's son had come to inquire about his father.

Joakim Sanders took him in and explained the violent attack that had just taken place.

— Thank you for your clarifications, he said. Do you know the people who brutalized my father? ... No.

I will leave you to your investigation and bring back my dog Magnus.

<>

Ayoub Zakaria after their accomplished crime found his accomplices Youssef and Amir:

— Well guys, I have Hitmann's personal data and his address. We'll be able to get him back to his place on Eugène Breton Street.

Gregory Hitmann was disoriented by the last 24 hours. It had started with Apache's illness.

The beautiful stallion was only a reflection of himself, he had found him lying in his stall, trembling and feverish. His urine was scanty and brown, with diarrhea and muscle pain, the veterinarian had established his diagnosis quickly: Leptospirosis, a disease carried by rodents, especially rat pee.

Two consequences were foreseen in this case, finding the origin of the infection, i.e. the rodents, and secondly, temporarily removing the sick horse from the infected cell.

A special stall for sick horses was located in a separate area, and Gregory was chosen as the patient guard.

And now that his father had been attacked in the nastiest of ways, he took Magnus back to his home and returned to watch over his favorite horse.

The three rascals who had attacked Roger went to Eugene Breton street in search of his home, they passed in front of the magician-mentalist Damien's establishment, immediately Ayoub Zakaria said *"it will be our next target, the magicians bring us luck!"*

The house was plunged into darkness, Magnus was awake and heard noises coming from the garden fence.

He had been trained not to move until the danger was imminent. He rose to his feet, all his senses alert, ready to pounce.

The three companions passed the fence and entered the garden adjoining a greenhouse, opened it and found garden tools:

— Great guys, we even have the means to enter the house by force, exclaimed Youssef.

— They like dogs on this property, look at that beautiful Doberman poster on the door says Amir.

— Well, I don't like dogs and they give it back to me, every time I get nudged, you'd think they're attracted to me, Ayoub shouted.

— We mustn't delay if we want to see the owner before he comes back, said Youssef.

Magnus remained on the lookout, following the progress of the thugs inside the house. They had broken a window in the basement and were climbing the stairs, thinking they were alone.

When they reached the living room, quiet as Baptiste, a black rocket rushed at Ayoub and tore off half his face, he collapsed in a spray of blood.

Youssef received the sixty kilos of muscles on his chest, and the last vision of the world he had was a huge row of fangs devouring his throat.

Amir had the presence of mind to close the living room door and return to the cellar.

He went out through the broken window and fell into the arms of Captain Joakim Sanders, who was warned by the silent alarm connected to the police station.

— Well, here is our friend Amir. Where are your two usual buddies? Unless you're going into solitaire now. By the look of your eyes, you've met a bigger bastard than you?

<>

Grégory Hitmann was not sleeping and stood at the bedside of the Apache gelding. The vet had just given him a vaccine *(the same as the one for dogs)* which was not very efficient but mainly to protect the other horses from the *leptospires* which settle in the liver and kidneys of the affected animals.

— Hello Mr. Hitmann, this is the police station of Blois, we intervened following the intrusion of thieves in your property, warned by your alarm system, they were the same robbers who had molested your father. They had kept the papers and knew your address.

But they were punished by your Doberman, who bit them and left the marks of his teeth in their flesh. They are not about to do it again.

Your father has come out of his coma and is recovering all his faculties.

You can come and pick up your dog tomorrow during the day. Damn animals! I guess he got back at me for not being able to protect Roger.

—Yes, continued Gregory, our Doberman is very attached to us, we weaned him ourselves, his parents had been hit by a car. We have been bottle-feeding him for about ten weeks, and he is a lovely dog when you get to know him, just don't touch us or get too close... if you value your balls!

— Yes, you have to tell that to your burglars, they told me about a devil all in black who had jumped on them. They confessed everything, even their past, present and future misdeeds. Magnus should join our dog teams, he would be a great recruit.

<>

Back at the stud, Gregory went directly to the veterinarians' hospital. Apache was doing much better and was standing upright, he neighed with joy when he saw Gregory.

The vet came to see him:
— The Squadron Leader wishes to congratulate you on your efforts to care for Apache.
He has authorized you to ride him on the royal horse track, reserved for ceremonial shows. All the gendarmes are there and will clap for you.

It is the first time that a lad has had so many honors, I congratulate you Grégory.

Chapter XV
Pacha, the French Bulldog

A revengeful dog and a horse cured of a serious illness, animals ready to do anything to please their master. The tour of France of animals attached to their owners was about to end and already Alex was leaving for a new adventure.

The Paris region deserved to be visited. Créteil and its artichoke towers called "Cabbages" attracted him like a magnet. The Ibis hotel at Carrefour Pompadour would be his haven of peace.

Aman Dar Salla lived a dark day. It began with the police bursting into his restaurant Pizzéria located on Verdun Avenue opposite the Intercommunal Hospital of Créteil.

At six o'clock, the legal time for searches, a swarm of uniforms with a *"Police"* armband had invaded his premises. His French bulldog Pacha had growled a few minutes before their arrival, sensing the hostility of the police.

Aman worked alone in his establishment, very proud of himself, he did not accept any advice from his friends about his lifestyle. He couldn't help but flirt with every woman passing by.

Complaints filed by sexually harassed waitresses were dismissed because Aman was cunning enough to carry out his acts without witnesses. In addition, he would shower the police station on nearby Oudry Boulevard with pizzas and other gifts.

This pizzeria was his second establishment. The previous one had been opened in 1980 in the fifteenth district, and Aman had already made friends with the police captain Ben Lafitte of the nearby police station, himself very interested in the weaker sex.
They were destined to meet each other.

Ben could not refuse him anything, one day he offered him a jacket labeled "police" with which Aman paraded in front of his conquests, whereas it was strictly forbidden to wear it in public, another day it was the telephone warning of Ben that a raid was likely to occur in his restaurant.

By dint of twisting indelicate arms and flirting with illegality, justice caught up with him on that September morning when he returned from vacation.

— Mr. Aman Dar Salla, I inform you of your rights and I inform you that you are in custody from now on, that is to say 6: 1/4 hours, and tie up your dog.

The lawyer Peche Delplanque, his office located near the Saint-Christophe Parish, Place de la Poste, received a phone call from the restaurant owner Aman, an old acquaintance, to come urgently to the police court to take his defense.

— What are the charges? he replied.

— The police didn't tell me anything, they took a jacket that Ben had given me and a Colt 45 that I used to defend myself in my restaurant, Aman continued.

I had told you over and over again to separate yourself from these objects.

— Captain Ben assured me that I had the right to have them in my home!

— No, the jacket you had no right to have it nor to bear it, you are not a policeman, that I know.

For the Colt 45, you have to obtain a permit to carry a special category 1 weapon of war and handgun, after having passed in a shooting center and having been sponsored by one of its members.

It is the Prefecture of the Department which delivers you the obtaining.

I am in immediate appearance, dear master, come, we are waiting for you?

On the other side of the courtroom, Monica Belcassem, a feverish young woman, was waiting for her hearing.

It was the accuser, she estimated to have been raped by the restaurant owner and claimed justice.

◇

Chaude Mayer, a faithful customer of the Pizzeria, was walking his dog Pinuts, a poodle with a black coat, that morning. His house adjoining the restaurant, he began his walk by coming to have a coffee with the owner.

He was surprised to see police cars parked in front of the establishment and even more surprised to see Aman come out in handcuffs.

— Chaude, my friend, can you take care of Pacha my dog. I don't understand what these policemen want from me. I'll be back promptly.

Mayer knew Aman's relationship with the police. Many times he had warned him that he was risking a lot by playing with fire. But this mule-headed man thought he was invulnerable, so this time he had to obey the law!

The two dogs went off to play in the leaves and bushes, oblivious to the quarrels of the humans.

At the court in Créteil, Peche the lawyer read the evidence against his client. He had escaped the complaints and the various sexual harassments, but now he was probably facing prison. The possession of the police jacket and the weapon could be defended but the rape of the young woman was more complicated.

First of all, it was necessary to reassure his client, as his sensitivity could take a big hit. The fear of prison dated back to his childhood in Egypt, where evil-doers ended up behind bars and were bludgeoned all day long.

He had avoided, until then, the promiscuity of the scoundrels locked up in French jails. Now he was going to taste it.

He had told her about the text messages and photos taken with his smartphone during his relationship with the young woman. Perhaps this will serve his defense.

On her side, Martine Bartolli, Monica Belcassem's lawyer, gathered the elements of the file and consulted the young woman:

— Well, Mrs. Belcassem, you have two children, one of whom is disabled. You spent the evening of Thursday, June 20 with Mr. Dar Salla.

After dinner, he took you to his room where he forced you to have sex. Then he dressed in a police jacket and threatened you with a gun if you turned him in. I've summed it up, haven't I?

— Yes master, he forced me to lie down and spread my legs!

— I don't need any further clarification! You can specify it at the hearing.

— Hearing 27 of September 3, the case of Belcassem against Dar Salla announced the clerk, the president Vincent Tran Van Phuc will lead the debates, please stand up.

The solemn atmosphere of the place frightened Ayman, who was trembling and starting to feel the fear of prison!

Peche Delplanque took his client's smartphone and presented it to President Van Phuc.

— Mr. Dar Salla wants to present you his laptop in which you will find the evidence of his innocence.

— Well, masters Bertolli and Delplanque, bring in your clients, he announced.

With these words, Aman Dar Salla collapsed in front of the courtroom, overcome by emotion.

President Van Phuc got up from his seat, surprised by the fainting of the accused, and seeing his paleness did not doubt his emotion.

— Commediante! Tragediante![22] laughed the lawyer Bertolli.

This did not please the president at all and made him the Remark:

— Calm down, Master, I am in a position to express myself on the events that are taking place in my courtroom.

We will resume the hearings in fifteen minutes.

Aman Dar Salla emerged from his brief pampering, and explained himself to the president:

I apologize, your honor, but during my Egyptian youth, my father was incarcerated in the jails of my country and was beaten like a plaster cast for his membership in the political opposition.

I confess that I had a sudden irrepressible fear of prison.

It was neither wanted nor premeditated, forgive me again!

— Okay, both of you, come closer. I just looked at Mr. Dar Salla's mobile phone.

Tell me, Mrs. Belcassem, do you remember the day after Mr. Salla's crime?

Uh no, your honor, she cried!

— Listen to Mrs. Belcassem, I have had enough emotions today, don't add to them by whining.

Immediately her tears dried up as if by magic.

The magistrate was smart enough to know what was real and what was not.

---

[22] Comedian, tragedian, quote from Pope Pius VII to Emperor Napoleon (1781).

— Well, Mrs. Belcassem, you tell me in the statement you made at the police station that you had not known this gentleman for a long time, that your children did not know him and that he had taken you by surprise.

This happened last year, perhaps your memories are still hazy, no?

Another thing, you don't remember the 21st of June, which is the music day, that Mr. Salla celebrated in his restaurant, after having supposedly sodomized you.

I see on this gentleman's mobile phone two text messages, dated June 21, where you end your sentence with *"I love you, my darling."*

Is this a kind word that one addresses to a person who raped you?

You tell me that your children did not know him, but I see a picture of your kids with this man's bulldog.

This little dog will put an end to your lies, Mrs. Belcassem. If there's one thing I can't stand, it's being laughed at! You will settle your marital disputes alone from now on.

As for the objects found at this gentleman's house, Captain Ben Lafitte was a little light on this one, his hierarchy will take care of his black sheep, because this jacket could be used for an assault.

The Colt 45 was never used, according to the instructions I received from the qualified persons of the Prefecture of Police, who verified it. It will be confiscated and destroyed.

Dear Masters, you will receive my conclusions within a month.

The lawyer took his client aside:

— It's the first time that the presence of a small dog in a police investigation has been dismissed, laughed Master Delplanque. You can thank Pacha who saved your ass and in what way! Mrs. Belcassem got stuck in her lies and the magistrate didn't like that at all.

Chapter XVI
Phoebus, the Fox

Alex left the dreadful towers of Créteil, asking himself the question *"would a dog causing a dismissal become the precedent in other judgments rendered?"*

The future will tell, he thought, in the meantime his journey was coming to an end, he decided to look at the city of Troyes, north-east of Paris. Not the one where Achilles the Trojan hero died from an arrow stuck in his tendon, but the old French medieval city, whose colorful half-timbered houses were built mostly in the XVIth century. The Ibis Budget hotel in the center of the city was the place to be.

The four companions had eaten and drank a lot from the dive bottle. Regulars of the Bougnat des Pouilles, this night bar in the city of Troyes, Gaston, Frederic, Jean and Goran started their evening with a pantagruelic meal and ended it in beauty in the nightclub *"Le Paparazzy."*

They had just robbed a tobacco shop in Riceys, using their car as a battering ram. They had taken the cash in hand with of course the cartons of cigarettes that they could resell on the sly, and scratch cards... for free.

— Word game after scratch game, laughed Gaston the gang leader.

◇

Georges Cimenon, his companion Martin Trevors and his son Philippe, found a flyer in their mailbox in the rue de Gournay in Troyes, plebiscising the cams of an educational farm in Méry sur Seine.

— Oh yes, Daddy, I'd like to discover the animals in the countryside.

The courts had long refused to recognize homosexual cohabitation, judging that it could only result from a relationship between a man and a woman. The law of November 15, 1999 expressly recognized the notion of homosexual cohabitation.

Thus, Martin Trevors and his son Philippe, born of a first marriage, had been in perfect love with Georges Cimenon for two years. A small and enthusiastic Fox terrier, named Phœbus *(god of the sun)* had come to join their blended family.

The opportunity to discover animals in the wild would be an excellent subject for documentation requested by the teacher of the Paradise Primary School, to their little Philippe. He had just turned six and was already acting like a real little man.

Having two dads didn't bother him more than that and when they came to pick him up at the end of school, accompanied by his Fox terrier, he said that Phœbus was his sunshine.

190

The four of them often went to the Parc de Fontaines where Phœbus could run to his heart's content. Martin and Georges would throw a frisbee at each other and the Fox would catch it in full flight, full of enthusiasm, and bring it back to Philippe, forcing him to participate in their games.

The four thugs had just gone wild on the dance-floor in the nightclub and the bouncer had asked them to leave the premises without delay.

— I will never understand this nightclub, we drop them a crazy amount of money and they don't want us to have fun, Gaston said.

— I have an idea, says Goran, I just received an advertisement about an educational farm that has just opened, with lots of animals to see.

— I don't like animals, continued Fred, they're full of fleas and they stink!

— Ditto for me, hiccupped Jean, whose drunkenness from the wine was making him aggressive. When I see an animal, it feels that I hate it and it comes at once to bite me.

— Well, guys, we've got a couple of packs of beer in the Twingo, we'll empty them on the spot.

All was quiet, the starry night seemed to hold its breath on the exactions which were going to take place in the farm of Méry.

Completely drunk, the four drunkards got out of the car with each one a pack of alcohol in the hand. The equestrian center transformed into an animal shelter was silent.

A sheep was bawling in displeasure at having Jean sitting on her back, Fred was smashing his bottles on the ducks that were running away, Gaston was trying to get the rabbits to drink alcohol, Goran was chasing the chickens and laughing like hell.

The night promised to be long for the poor animals.

<>

Georges, Martin and Philippe had arrived in front of the entrance to the Méry-sur-Seine leisure lodge, which houses the educational farm. A strange impression of abandonment reigned on the spot.

Police and firemen vehicles were parked in front of the entrance.

Through the bars of the gate, Georges and Martin could see feathers scattered along the path leading to the cages, dead rabbits were hanging on the fence, a bloody ewe was dragging lamentably.

Something dramatic had happened, and so they backed up and returned to their car parked in the parking lot near the Seine.

— Philippe, don't move from the Renault Mégane : the police ask us for our papers. The animals were martyred last night. We will visit the farm another time!

Georges and Martin were answering precise questions from the investigators. Apparently some people didn't like animals in the area! A Renault Twingo had been left behind, full of garbage and dead alcohol bottles. Stolen the night before, the forensic police were taking prints. No doubt that the robbers will be quickly found.

Suddenly Phœbus, all wet and screaming for death, ran into the premises of the cottage. Sensing a problem, Georges and Martin followed him into an empty parking lot, their Renault had disappeared.

192

Leaning over the quay, they saw her floating between two waters.

Georges could not swim, so Martin dived in and pulled out his son. The firemen on the spot gave him artificial respiration and revived him.

Thanks to a little black and white ball of fur, Philippe was rescued.

◇

In the newspaper *"L'express,"* the headline read:
"Animals killed in an educational farm, some survived this Sunday."

Four minors aged 16 to 18 were arrested after the discovery earlier this week of several slaughtered animals in a former equestrian center in Méry-sur-Seine.

According to the Est éclair, these four young people reside in the Aube department and are to be presented to a juvenile judge this Thursday.

On Monday an employee of the farm had the horror of finding that out of the twenty or so animals that were in the establishment, only six were still alive.

A sheep, a rabbit, ducks, but also other birds, had been found dead and their bodies showed marks of torture.

According to France 3 Grand Est, sticks and beer cans were found on the spot[23].

---

[23] Report France 3 Champagne-Ardenne

How can some people inflict abuse and torture on defenseless animals simply for fun or games?

Alex was disappointed by so much wickedness. Maybe his regional investigations in the four corners of the Hexagon, will put these torturers in front of their responsibilities.

Conclusion

A dog participating in the rescue of his master, nothing but very ordinary, for him God exists and he holds him on a leash.

There are people, insensitive to the animal cause, who take a cat or a dog for a few months and get rid of it when the vacations come.

Alex was going through the different editorials written during his expedition in the deepest France, the one of rich or poor people all animated by this insane love towards their favorite animal, a feeling so intense that the animal would come to let itself die on the grave of its master at his death.

There are signs that show the love between an animal and its owner;

When he celebrates when you come home, even after a few minutes of absence, he wags his tail, licks you, jumps on you, runs around, sometimes barks to show you the joy of finding you;

When he comes to snuggle with you, it is because he considers you as his pillar and your presence calms him;

When he licks you it is to reassure you, he felt your tensions, your worries, your doggie is a real sponge;

When he yawns at the same time as you, it is because he feels empathy and it is his way of showing it to you;

When he sleeps next to you, it's because your fur ball trusts you and he feels that you are able to watch over him and also to protect him in case of danger; When he gives you a hug after the meal, it is a great sign of affection, he does not try to have a candy because he is already full;

When he steals your dirty clothes to store them in his basket, it means that he is looking for your smell when you are away;

When he brings you his favorite toy, it's because he wants to play with you and also it's a mark of confidence, since he entrusts you with what is most dear to him,

When he lets you stroke his belly, it's the ultimate sign of submission and trust, tolerated only with his master, if he lies on his back, all four paws in the air and looks you straight in the eyes, waiting for a caress, it's because he knows that you won't hurt him;

When he protects your house, it means that he is concerned about his territory and his family, every stranger represents a danger that must be scared away;

When he takes care of you, if you are sick, sad, worried, your pet is very receptive, feels it and shows you his compassion by snuggling up to you while you get better;

When he watches you leave quietly, this behavior is very positive, it means that he has full confidence in you and he knows that you will come back, so why worry?[24]

Sometimes all it takes is an exchange of glances between a dog and its owner to feel the strong bond that unites them to each other. Based on this observation, Japanese researchers, whose

---

[24] Report 380 millions of friends.

work was published in the very serious American magazine *Science* in 2015, managed to demonstrate that when humans and dogs look each other in the eye, the level of oxytocin increases significantly for each.

This typical love hormone appears for example when a mother looks at her child.

The intense connection that all owners feel for their dogs is therefore scientifically proven, if it were needed!

This is also the reason why pet therapy is so effective with people suffering from autism or post-traumatic stress[25].

---

[25] Animalaxy Survey.